TERROR BEGINS
AT HOME

Claire Bartel, like every other young mother, is desperately in need of someone to babysit. So when beautiful, sweet-natured nanny Peyton Flanders shows up on Claire's doorstep full of wonderful advice and flashing a trustworthy smile, she seems like the ideal answer to an overworked parent's prayers. But soon chilling, vengeful things begin to happen. . . . The baby loses all interest in Claire. . . . Her young daughter becomes secretive. . . . Her husband grows cold. . . . And her friends meet with horrifying accidents. The Bartels' new nanny is anything but a godsend. Who is this angel-faced menace with the deadly power to terrorize Claire's tranquil family life? What is her evil secret that makes Claire's heart race with fear? . . .

THE
HAND
THAT ROCKS

H THE AND
THAT ROCKS
THE
CRADLE

A Novel by Robert Tine

Based on the Motion Picture from Hollywood Pictures

Executive Producers Ted Field, Rick Jaffa and Robert W. Cort

Based on the Screenplay Written by Amanda Silver
Produced by David Madden
Directed by Curtis Hanson

A SIGNET BOOK

SIGNET
Published by the Penguin Group
Penguin Books USA Inc., 375 Hudson Street,
New York, New York 10014, U.S.A.
Penguin Books Ltd, 27 Wrights Lane,
London W8 5TZ, England
Penguin Books Australia Ltd, Ringwood,
Victoria, Australia
Penguin Books Canada Ltd, 10 Alcorn Avenue,
Toronto, Ontario, Canada M4V 3B2
Penguin Books (N.Z.) Ltd, 182–190 Wairau Road,
Auckland 10, New Zealand

Penguin Books Ltd, Registered Offices:
Harmondsworth, Middlesex, England

First published by Signet, an imprint of New American Library, a division of
Penguin Books USA Inc.

First Printing, July, 1992
10 9 8 7 6 5 4 3 2 1

 REGISTERED TRADEMARK—MARCA REGISTRADA

PRINTED IN THE UNITED STATES OF AMERICA

Photos by Matthew McVay

PUBLISHER'S NOTE
This is a work of fiction. Names, characters, places, and incidents either are the
product of the author's imagination or are used fictitiously, and any resemblance
to actual persons, living or dead, events, or locales is entirely coincidental.

H<small>THE</small>AND
THAT ROCKS
<small>THE</small>
CRADLE

CHAPTER 1

He rode the bicycle so slowly it seemed that he was in constant danger of keeling over. The wagon attached to the rear fender appeared to steady him, acting as both keel and rudder. The bike was old, dented, and rusty, its green paint flaking. It and its rider looked curiously out of place in that neighborhood, Madison Park, an old and established upper-middle-class area just a few miles from downtown Seattle.

When bicycles were seen in Madison Park streets, they were shiny ten-speeds ridden by health-conscious adults or brightly colored models sporting training wheels. The riders, adults or children, were almost always white. The young man slowly pedaling his broken-down bicycle up the steep hill was black. His clothing was as old and as down-at-the-heel as his bicycle. The overalls he wore had been khaki once, a long time ago, but now were so covered with paint and grease stains that the original color could only be seen in a couple of brown patches. His hooded sweatshirt had been washed so many times that it had faded from a rich crimson to a washed-out pink. There were ragged holes in his old black high-top sneakers, the laces in knots. Even the Seattle Mariners cap on his head was battered, the bill creased down the middle.

He had never been in this neighborhood before and he looked about him with curiosity. The houses on the tree-lined street were old and well built and they sat on generous parcels of land. Gardens were prim and well cared for, lawns were trimmed precisely and seemed to glow a fresh green. There was a hint of salt spray in the air.

The man allowed the bike to roll to a halt in front of one house and pulled a piece of paper from the pocket of his sweatshirt. He compared the numbers scrawled there with the numbers posted on the gate of a house. This was it.

He smiled as he examined the house. It was a stout old Victorian, built at the turn of the century, and made to last forever. It had a high-peaked shingled roof with tall upper-story windows and delicate latticework trim. A wide, shady wraparound porch sported carved pillars and an ornate railing. He ran a practiced eye over the whole building and could not see much wrong with it, other than the fact that it could have used a little paint here and there, mostly on the trim.

He dismounted, carefully propped his bike up on its kickstand, mounted the front steps, and rang the doorbell. Although he could not hear it ring deep within the house, he could hear other sounds. A television was on somewhere, and beyond that, the sound of two voices. A man and a little girl. They were singing.

"I am the captain of the *Pinafore*," sang the man.

"And a right good captain, too," sang the little girl.

He pushed the doorbell again.

"You're very, very good, but be it understood, I command a right good crew," sang the man.

"We're very, very good, but be it understood, he commands a right good crew," agreed the little girl.

Plainly no one had heard the doorbell. He stepped off the porch and walked around the side of the house, peering in the windows as he went. The interior of the house was both stylish and comfortable, neat but not obsessively so. Toys were scattered across the floor in the family room, and yesterday's newspaper lay crumpled on a sofa.

The furniture was as well made as the house itself. There were dark, upholstered armchairs and wooden Mission pieces. The coffee table in one room was large and round, a disk of lightly finished maple. On the oak-plank floors, stained dark and polished to a high shine, were rough-weave Indian rugs, shot through with colorful and varied patterns. A tall, cherrywood grandfather clock ticked solemnly in the corner. A profusion of houseplants hung in the windows, stood in earthen pots on tables, or sat in large copper planters on the floor.

The singing continued with brio, louder now that he was at the side of the house. "And Father, if I may, you'll occasionally say, I'm never, never, sick at sea!"

"What never?"

"No never!"

"What *never*?"

"Well, *hardly* ever!"

He was staring in the kitchen window now. A young woman was moving around the room. She was smiling to herself, as if pleased that her husband and daughter, upstairs, could enjoy something as simple as a Gilbert and Sullivan song together. Upended in a corner of kitchen, in an island of newspapers, was a rocking chair. The old paint had been stripped off, revealing the light wood.

The woman was very pretty, with large dark eyes and black hair cut short to her collar. Under her baggy sweatshirt and pants he could see that she was heavily pregnant. She poured three glasses of juice.

There was a large, antique refectory table in the middle of the room and three places had been set at it. The walls were wood-paneled and the floors covered with dark terra-cotta tiles. He noticed that a number of brightly colored children's paintings were stuck to the refrigerator door with magnets. Hanging from a rack over the stove were a dozen large pots and pans, their copper bottoms gleaming.

The singing was even louder now. The voices were resonant and cheerful. Neither was a great singer, but they seemed to sing out of pure enjoyment. "He's hardly ever sick at sea. . . . So give three cheers and one cheer more for the hardy captain of the *Pinafore!*"

He was at the backdoor now and was about to knock when the woman saw him, dropped the juice carton, and screamed. Orange juice pooled at her feet and ran across the tile floor. She backed away from the door.

Her scream started a chain reaction. The man outside jumped, put his hands to his ears, terrified. He closed his eyes tightly and howled.

The singing upstairs stopped abruptly. An instant later a man appeared dressed only in his pajama bottoms. A little girl ran right behind him.

For a second the man outside couldn't move, as if he was rooted to the spot.

"Hey, you!" shouted the man in the kitchen. "What are you doing here?"

The sound of the man's voice seemed to shoot through him, giving him the power to move. He took to his heels, running for the street. The man inside the house shadowed him, watching through the windows. Then the man of the house intercepted him on the porch, standing between him and the gate, blocking his path to the street and his bicycle.

The frightened man stopped, his eyes wide with fear, and threw up his hands as if to protect himself. "Don't hurt me," he said, his voice shaking.

"Who are you?"

He opened his mouth and tried to speak, struggling with a painful stammer. Finally he managed to gasp out one word: "Solomon."

"What are you doing here?"

With trembling hands, he pulled a piece of paper from his pocket. The other man scanned it quickly and his face fell. The black man watched him, worry and fear mingling with the shyness of his expression. He was sure he was in terrible trouble.

"I'm sorry," the man from the house said. "Very sorry."

Solomon shrugged. His eyes were downcast, as if he was intently studying the boards of the porch floor at his feet.

The man extended his hand and Solomon took it and they shook. His palm was rough and callused, as if he had done manual labor every day of his life. The white man's hand was softer and smaller.

"I'm Michael Bartel," he said. "I didn't mean to scare you. I'm sorry. Please come in." He opened the door and guided Solomon to the kitchen. Solomon walked through the rooms carefully, as if he was afraid of breaking something simply by being there.

The woman and the child were still in the kitchen, the child half-hidden behind and clutching at her mother, peeping out at the stranger. Although the man had frightened them all, the little girl decided she liked his open, serious face. He noticed that the orange juice had been mopped up quickly. He felt better about that.

"Honey," said Michael Bartel, "this gentleman says that the Better Way Society sent him."

"Better Day," corrected Solomon solemnly.

"Sorry. Better Day Society."

Solomon spoke, managing to conquer his stammer. "The Better Day Society helps place the mentally disabled with employment opportunities." He spoke as if he had learned this little speech by heart. "I live there." The last three words seemed to come from the heart, not memorized like the rest.

The little girl smiled at him. He smiled back, a wide, happy smile. He seemed less nervous now, as if no longer afraid of being punished.

Mrs. Bartel looked relieved. "Of course. You're here to build the fence!"

"I tried ringing the bell at the front door," said Solomon in his own defense. "I didn't mean to frighten anyone. I hope you're not mad at me."

"We're not mad at you. We're the ones who should be apologizing. I'm sorry." Mrs. Bartel took a step toward him. Her smile was reassuring and it calmed him immeasurably. "We couldn't hear a thing—not with all that Gilbert and Sullivan."

"Who," asked Solomon, "are they?"

"The singing," said Mrs. Bartel. "I'm Claire." She pulled her daughter up next to her. "And this is Emma."

Emma was dark like her mother, with her hair cut in a little pageboy. Her most charming feature was her round dark eyes, which always seemed to be on the verge of crinkling with laughter.

"It is very nice to make your acquaintance, Emma." Very gravely Solomon shook the little girl's hand.

"I'm going to put on some shoes," said Claire, "so I can show Solomon around outside. Emma, see if our guest would like anything to drink."

Emma nodded. "My mom says to ask if you want anything."

Solomon thought for a moment. There was something he wanted very much and so he told her. "I would like a new red bicycle," he said very seriously. "With a big basket on the handlebars."

Emma nodded, understanding him perfectly. "That sounds really neat. But how about something to drink? Do you like orange juice?"

Solomon didn't want to be reminded of orange juice right at that moment. His eyes settled on the coffeemaker. "I would rather have coffee, if that's not too much trouble."

"Coming right up," said Emma. She poured him a cup of coffee from the pot standing on the counter. "Milk and sugar?"

"No, thank you."

Solomon examined the rocker in the corner of the room. It was an old piece of furniture with well-turned wood and good tight joints. He nodded approvingly, brushing his big fingers across the smooth wood. "It's a good job," he said knowingly.

"We're having a baby," announced Emma. "Mom's giving it my rocking chair."

Solomon nodded somberly. "You must be very proud. Rocking is very important."

"You think so?" asked Emma.

"I know so," he replied.

The Bartels returned to the kitchen. Claire had slipped on a pair of running shoes and her husband wore jeans and a sweatshirt.

"Ready?"

"Yes, ma'am."

They walked outside and Solomon went straight to the old, rusted chain-link fence that surrounded the property. He examined it closely, his face very serious. He rocked the posts in the ground and found them loose and he strummed the chain as if it were a musical instrument, badly out of tune.

A bright yellow school bus pulled up to the Bartel house, but Solomon scarcely noticed it. He didn't even look up when the horn honked loudly.

"There's your bus, Emma," said Michael.

"I have to go to school now, Solomon," said Emma, racing up to the house for her book bag.

"Don't forget your jacket," shouted her mother.

"Oh, yeah!" Emma burst through the backdoor and emerged through the front a moment later, clutching her backpack and raincoat.

"Good luck with the play rehearsal this afternoon!" her father called.

"Bye!" shouted Emma. She hopped on the bus and the doors closed with a hiss.

Solomon had never taken his eyes off the Cyclone fence during all this. He still stared hard at it, but he didn't seem to be seeing it, instead he seemed to be concentrating on a vision of the new fence.

"Okay," he said finally. "I see." He walked a few steps. "You want it to end here."

"Well, no," said Claire uncertainly. She was not sure she wasn't about to hurt his feelings by correcting him. She had as clear a vision of what the fence should look like as Solomon did.

It was her delicate task to get him to understand exactly what she wanted.

"Well, no, not exactly. The fence should contain the whole area, but the gate should be here." She pointed to the spot where the present gate stood.

Solomon thought for a moment. He had one very important question. "Do you want this fence to keep people in or keep people out?"

It was, to say the least, an odd question. Claire and Michael exchanged a worried look. Michael thought this whole thing was crazy and hoped that his wife wasn't serious about hiring this very strange young man.

Claire was not as quickly put off as her husband and did her best to sound understanding. "Well," she said evenly, "both, I suppose. I guess it should mostly keep people out."

Solomon nodded knowingly, as if digesting her answer. He gazed across the yard toward the house, taking in the whole scene. He sighed and smiled happily. Solomon had never had a home of his own and he savored houses and families more than other people, who took such commonplace things for granted.

"This is a good place," he said quietly. "Some homes have all the heart."

Claire smiled. "I suppose they do."

"Now I'll measure." He spread his arms wide

and then began taking short steps along the inside perimeter of the fence as if walking a tightrope. He counted off his steps in a loud voice. "One, two, five, nine . . ."

Michael looked to his wife in disbelief. This was too much. The question about the purpose of the fence could have been dismissed as mere eccentricity, but the man couldn't even count. Michael wasn't sure about hiring someone from the Better Day Society in the first place, and this kind of behavior confirmed his doubts. He was about to say something when Solomon stopped counting.

He turned to the Bartels, a wide grin on his face. His eyes were bright with good humor. "Just kidding." His big hands patted down his pockets, as if he were looking for something. He pulled a bright silvery object from the paint-stained overalls he wore under his sweatshirt. "I have a tape measure." He displayed the big, seventy-five-foot tape measure.

Claire laughed and Michael looked somewhat relieved. Now he knew it was a joke, but he remained doubtful about the wisdom of hiring Solomon.

"I have to get ready for work," said Michael. He started toward the house.

"So everything's okay out here?" asked Claire.

"Right as rain," said Solomon with a small smile.

"Give a yell if you need anything." Claire took her husband by the arm and pulled him toward the house. She liked Solomon. He had a sense of humor.

Once inside, Michael gave voice to his concerns. While he got dressed he watched Solomon through the upstairs window of their bedroom. "I don't know," he said doubtfully, knotting a tie at his throat. "Do you think he's the right guy for the job? After all, a fence is a very complicated thing to build. I'm not sure . . ."

Claire was seated at the vanity, staring at her reflection in the mirror as she applied a little powder to her cheeks. "Oh, Michael, I don't think it's worth worrying about. The people at Better Day told me that Solomon has plenty of experience in construction. And I'll be here. I'll be overseeing him the whole time."

Michael remained unconvinced. He turned away from the window, folding his arms across his chest. "Even so. It's not the most practical idea to have a mentally disabled person building us a fence. It has to be level, secure, well planned. . . ."

"Disabled people deserve the opportunity to

contribute, Michael," said Claire a little sharply.

"I'm all for them contributing," he protested, "but do they have to contribute on our fence?"

"If he knows how to do it, why not let him have the chance? The Better Day Society wouldn't have sent him if they didn't have confidence in him."

Michael still did not look convinced and he made one last-ditch attempt to change his wife's mind. "Look. Wouldn't it be easier to just donate a couple of hundred dollars to the society and call it a day?"

Claire nodded shortly. "Yes. I suppose that would be much easier." She turned big dark brown eyes on her husband, telegraphing a look that was at once disapproving and amused.

Michael shrugged. "Okay, okay, you win. Just don't give me that look. I can't stand it."

Claire smiled warmly and walked to her husband. "That's my man."

She pulled his face down to hers and kissed him long and softly on the lips. His hands circled around her, running across her swollen stomach.

"How are you feeling, angel?"

"Right as rain," she murmured.

He kissed her neck delicately, nuzzling her soft skin.

Claire stretched under his touch and shivered deliciously.

"Mmm." She sighed. "I didn't know that scientists were such good kissers."

"I didn't know that pregnant women were so sexy." He lifted her up and laid her gently on the big double bed.

"Well, think again. . . ."

CHAPTER 2

It was widely believed in Seattle that Dr. Victor Mott was among the best OB/GYN specialists in the city, a man so respected that Claire Bartel felt lucky to have become his patient so far into her second pregnancy. Dr. Mott's waiting room spoke volumes about his practice. It seemed to exude money, comfort, and prestige. It was ultramodern and luxurious in an understated, tasteful way. The couches were low-slung, Italian creations of leather and steel, and the magazines fanning out on the elegant coffee tables ran the gamut from *American Baby* to French *Vogue*.

The clientele, six or eight other women of Claire's age, all of them reading magazines as they awaited their turns, seemed to match the decor. There were other doctors in the practice, but Victor Mott was considered the star.

All the women were well coiffed and made up, and so stylishly dressed that Claire felt slightly scruffy, dowdy even, in her pregnancy blue jeans, sneakers, and Land's End barn jacket. It didn't make her feel any better when she noticed that every time a newcomer entered the room, the women already waiting there subjected her to a close scrutiny, evaluating her maternity outfit, shoes, and accessories. Claire could only imagine what they thought of her. Of course, they couldn't know that she planned to return to her volunteer job at the Seattle Botanical Gardens immediately after her checkup with the illustrious Dr. Mott.

She flipped through her copy of *Parenting* magazine uneasily, anxious to get through her exam and out in the open air again. No place made her happier than the Botanical Gardens and no place unnerved her quite as much as a doctor's office. She was sorry that her first obstetrician had retired. She had trusted him and thought it would have been nice to have him deliver both her children.

Claire was relieved when the nurse finally called, "Mrs. Bartel?"

"That's me." She stood up and followed the nurse into one of the examining rooms.

The nurse reassured her somewhat. Given the chic waiting room, Claire expected equally chic nurses, but Dr. Mott's tended to be older, field-hockey-coach types.

This one sat Claire on a steel examining table, slipped a blood-pressure cuff around her arm, and pumped it up.

Staring at the pressure gauge over half-frame glasses, she asked, "This is your first exam with Dr. Mott?"

Claire nodded. "Yes. The doctor who delivered my first baby retired and Dr. Mott was nice enough to take me on midterm."

"Well," the nurse said briskly, "he's one of the best." She ripped the cuff off Claire's arm. "Expecting his own, you know. He's going to be a father himself in a couple of months."

"I didn't know that."

The nurse gave her a paper gown. "Take everything off." Her instructions were business-like. "Put the gown on, open at the front."

Claire stripped off her clothes quickly, donned the gown, then sat down to wait. She hated these long boring waits and felt self-conscious and vulnerable in the paper robe. After ten minutes she jumped slightly when the door opened and the doctor came in accompanied by the nurse.

"How are we today, Mrs. Bartel?" Dr. Mott was a tall, burly, handsome man in his forties with a full head of wavy blond hair and a mouthful of large white teeth. He smiled easily, his eyes crinkling in good humor. His easygoing manner made him seem younger than he actually was as his blue eyes flitted across her open gown.

"I'm just fine," said Claire. "The baby's been kicking up a storm."

Dr. Mott didn't seem to be much interested. He was scanning her chart. The nurse bustled in the background, laying out instruments on a sterile cloth.

"Let's see. . . . You have asthma. Any trouble with it so far?"

Claire shook her head. "No. It flares up, but only rarely these days. Usually it's stress-related."

He put the chart aside. "Good. Let's have a look." He tapped the stirrups on the edge of the table. "Feet up." He turned to pull a latex glove from a box.

For a moment Claire looked reluctant to put her feet in the stirrups. "I didn't know it was usual to give pelvic exams after the third month."

Dr. Mott flashed his teeth at Claire. "Oh," he explained, "we don't usually do pelvics again until week thirty-six. But I like to give all my new patients a full exam on the first visit."

Claire nodded and slid down on the table, resting her feet in the cold metal stirrups. He was the doctor, after all, and the explanation made perfect sense.

The telephone affixed to the wall beeped discreetly and the nurse answered it quickly. "Yes?" She listened a moment, then turned to Dr. Mott. "It's Mrs. Miller, doctor. She's calling again for test results."

The doctor's eyes were fastened on the rounded swell of Claire's breasts, just visible through the gaps in her ill-fitting robe. She felt his look and tried to stretch the paper to cover herself.

Dr. Mott seemed to have a little trouble pulling his eyes away and he didn't seem to have comprehended exactly what his nurse had said to him. His eyes were locked on Claire and it made her feel the slightest bit uncomfortable.

Finally he turned. "Who did you say it was?"

"Mrs. Miller, doctor."

Mott nodded to himself, as if recalling the patient. "Why don't you go ahead and give them to her, Maria. She's all clear. If she has questions, tell her I'll call her back later. Probably sometime this afternoon."

"Yes, doctor."

"The files are in my office. And while you're in there, would you please call the lab for the result of yesterday's Virupaps?"

The nurse nodded and left the room.

Dr. Mott walked around the table and leaned down over Claire. He untied the laces of the gown and pushed aside the material. He touched her breasts, allowing the fingers to linger a split second longer than was strictly necessary. Then, with a light circular motion, he began pressing on them. When his fingers brushed gently across her nipples, Claire looked into his face, watching as he closed his eyes and his breathing became deeper. He could have been concentrating. . . .

She wriggled under his touch, distinctly uncomfortable, blood rushing to her cheeks. He seemed to sense her disquiet.

"Am I hurting you?" he whispered.

"No," said Claire.

"Good . . . Good . . ."

He continued feeling her breasts, but Claire sensed that his touch was changing. She fought a moment's panic, telling herself that she was imagining things. Inadvertently she shifted uncomfortably and her sudden move seemed to rouse Dr. Mott.

He opened his eyes, but his hand remained on her breast.

"You're doing just fine," he said, his voice slightly husky, then moved to the foot of the table.

Prone on the table, her knees up, her feet hooked into the stirrups, the gown stretched taut between her legs, like a tent, Claire could not see the doctor's hands.

Unobserved, he slid off the surgical glove and slowly inserted one, then two fingers, sliding them slowly and methodically in and out. Claire jumped and grimaced.

"Cold?"

"A little," she managed to stammer.

"Try to relax."

He moved his fingers in and out of her, his other hand stroking her belly, going through the motions of palpating her cervix and uterus. Claire had undergone pelvic exams before and they were never pleasant, but there was something about this one that seemed out of the ordinary. Dr. Mott was not going about the exam in the usual brisk, efficient way of other doctors. This was more sensuous than clinical, a caress rather than an examination.

Sweat broke out on Claire's upper lip. She

stared at the soundproofing in the ceiling, fighting the panic rising within her. She bit her lip and her eyes closed suddenly and tightly.

"That's just fine. . . . Just fine," said Dr. Mott, his voice thick and throaty. "Just fine. Just perfect . . ."

The chic women in the waiting room looked up as Claire walked quickly for the door. Every one of them could see the panic on her face. It could only mean one thing: bad news. A complication, a poor test result. The nightmare of every pregnant woman. A couple of them touched their bellies, as if rubbing talismans, warding off bad luck.

"Mrs. Bartel!" called the receptionist.

Claire walked on as if she hadn't heard.

"Mrs. Bartel! We have to schedule your next—"

But Claire was out the door. On the escalator to the underground parking lot, she felt the first, unmistakable twinge of an asthma attack. As if metal bands were tightening across her, she felt her lungs constrict.

Her chest rose and fell and panic began building within her. She felt herself choking, unable to suck any breath into her lungs. A terrifying sense of helplessness overcame her as the asthma seized her completely. Her lungs felt inflated and empty at the same time. The breath broke loud and tortured in her throat and she wheezed and gagged.

She scrabbled frantically in her purse for her inhaler and aimed the barrel at her mouth. The small puff of bitter medicine hit the back of her throat and she sucked it as deep as she could into her lungs.

Gradually the wheezing diminished, but the fearful sense of being unable to breathe remained. Her legs felt weak and rubbery, her head dizzy.

She did her best to calm herself, focusing her diminished energy on a single thought: escape.

CHAPTER 3

Claire stood under the pounding hot water of the shower, scrubbing herself in a frenzied, almost hysterical way, as if she were expunging the memory along with the dirt and shame. She could still feel his hands on her, could still hear his heavy breathing.

The warm water was good and cleansing. As it pounded down she could feel herself growing calmer—slightly—relieved that she had managed to get herself home and into the shower without becoming hysterical.

She stepped out of the shower and swathed herself in two thick towels, using another to gather her wet hair. She leaned against the sink and sighed deeply. Even though she was safe in her own home and a little more composed, she was still nervous. She could not quite believe what had happened in Dr. Mott's office.

She could still see the look of surprise on his face when she suddenly closed her legs and jumped off the table. She had said nothing to him, no word of protest. She had merely made up a story about having an urgent appointment that she had just remembered. Both she and he knew that few things were more important to a pregnant woman than a doctor's appointment, but he went along with the fiction. Both of them had known what was going on. He did not attempt to apologize. . . .

Claire wiped the steam from the bathroom mirror and stared at herself for a moment, then closed her eyes, resting her forehead on the cool, damp glass. A headache pounded just behind her eyes, the aftermath of the asthma attack and the incident in the doctor's office. She felt exhausted, emotionally drained, sick to her stomach.

"Claire?"

She jumped and turned. In the doorway of the bathroom, her husband was looking at her curiously, aware that something was wrong. Her usually rosy face was pale and drawn, her eyes dull with pain and worry.

"Michael! You scared me."

"Are you all right?"

Claire always tried to be a tower of strength, never admitting weakness, not even to her husband. She tried to nod yes, but the weight of her jangled nerves and emotions overcame her.

"Oh, Michael . . ." Her voice was tinged with tears.

"What? What happened? The baby?"

Claire shook her head. "No, the baby is fine. It's me."

"Claire—"

She fell into her husband's arms, sobbing and shuddering. Her tears were hot and bitter.

She cried in his arms for a few minutes, wallowing for a moment in her misery. Gradually the tears dried up and she felt even more exhausted than she had before. Slowly and with difficulty she managed to pull herself together.

Michael led her to the bed and she collapsed on it, curling herself into a protective ball.

Michael stroked her hair tenderly. "You have to tell me exactly what happened."

She turned her tear-streaked face to his. "Michael . . . I just want to forget all about it."

"Please, Claire. It's important."

Slowly, haltingly at first, she told her husband of her encounter with Dr. Mott. Michael paced the room, fighting to quell his rising anger.

"It was the *way* he was touching me," she said vehemently. "It started with the breast exam. . . . It was like he was caressing me. And then his voice . . . It was . . . His voice was different . . . provocative."

"Provocative?" Michael asked.

Claire tried to re-create the moment, battling with her disgust and her natural tendency to try to block out a painful memory.

"It was as if he—as if he were . . . getting off. Getting off on examining me." For a moment it seemed as if her tears would come swelling to the surface again. "I'm not absolutely positive, but when he stood up, I think . . . I think he had an erection."

Michael stopped pacing. "What?" he shouted angrily.

"Michael, you promised to stay calm!"

He took a deep breath, fighting to stay in control. "Okay, okay. I'm calm." He paused a moment. "Did he . . . you didn't try to run, or scream, or anything like that?"

"I was scared," said Claire plaintively. "I didn't know what to do."

"Did you think he might hurt you?"

"I don't *know*. I just got out of there as fast as I could. He knew I was upset, but he didn't say anything."

"You have to file a complaint," said Michael flatly.

Claire paled and felt herself getting dizzy. A complaint would just stir things up. There might even be publicity.

"No!" she cried. "I just can't be *sure*." Her eyes darted around the room, as if she wanted to look anywhere but at her angry husband.

"Claire, you have to."

"He's such a prominent doctor, Michael! I mean, what if I was wrong? What if I accused him and I was wrong about the whole thing? I could destroy him. He would be ruined for no reason at all." Even as she spoke, though, she knew there was no mistake. She knew what had happened and so did Dr. Victor Mott. She was denying it because she couldn't bring herself to face it.

Michael paused a long moment. "Are you sure now?" He knew his wife would never make wild accusations. If Claire thought she had been molested, then she definitely had been.

Claire nodded. "Yes," she said quietly.

"Then we have to file a complaint."

Claire's frail composure began to crumble. "No, Michael. I can't."

Michael sat down on the bed and took his wife in his arms, pressing her close to his chest and rocking her like a child. His mouth was close to her ear. "If we don't report this to the medical-ethics board, he is going to do the same thing to someone else. You have to trust yourself, honey."

"I don't know if I can do it, Michael. I just don't know."

"I'll be right with you the whole time. We'll go through it together."

"Oh, God," said Claire miserably. "Why did this have to happen?"

"It won't happen again," he said softly. "I'm proud of you, honey. You're doing the right thing. . . ."

Hundreds, perhaps thousands of times in the following weeks, Claire Bartel had reason to ask herself if she had, in fact, done the right thing. The process of reporting Dr. Mott's misconduct was low-key at first, but then as newspapers and TV got hold of the story Claire found herself at the center of a steadily escalating controversy.

More and more she withdrew into her home, her family, islands of peace in the middle of a media storm. True to his word, Michael stood beside her every step of the way and together they maintained a steadfast dignity.

The initial complaint was relatively easy. She went to the appropriate authorities and made a statement and had it notarized. The officials at the medical-ethics review board said that they would examine her statement and get back to her. In a matter of days they did, along with a document from Mott refuting her charges, stating in medicalese just what had happened in the examination room that day.

Claire had wanted to drop the matter there, but Michael insisted, angry now that Mott had not only molested his wife, but was also calling her a liar.

Somehow the newspapers got hold of the story and, given Mott's prominence, gave it a lot of attention. The next few weeks were a blur of hearings and depositions, threats of lawsuits and countersuits, but the legal machinery ground on inexorably. . . .

Dr. Victor Mott drank the cognac in the big balloon snifter, looking over the rim at the newscaster on the wide-screen television set in his study.

The scene shifted and he saw his own face smiling out at the world. The picture had been taken at some medical banquet, and he looked the very image of a successful doctor. Faultlessly cut dinner jacket, perfectly knotted black tie at his throat.

"Dr. Victor Mott, prominent Seattle gynecologist and obstetrician, was indicted today by the district attorney's office. . . . The scandal began when one of Mott's pregnant patients went to the state medical board claiming that she had been sexually molested by the doctor during an examination."

Claire's frightened face now appeared on the screen. The doctor sipped and remembered how she had fled from the office. He recalled being worried at the time but then dismissing his fears. She wouldn't say anything, he had told himself, none of the others had.

"Since the patient's initial accusation, four more women have come forward alleging that they, too, had been sexually molested while under Mott's care."

And that, thought Dr. Mott, was the end. If Bartel had been the only one, then he could have beaten the charges—his word against the word of a hysterical, pregnant woman.

"Citing the possibility of criminal misdeeds, the state medical board passed the case on to the district attorney's office, which today secured seven indictments against Dr. Mott."

Criminal misdeeds. The words seemed to burn into his brain. The disgrace, the loss of his practice, he could have stood all that. But the possibility of jail . . . He could not even think about it. There was only one thing to do. Only one thing he *could* do.

With a weary sigh he finished the cognac and put the expensive goblet down carefully. He opened a desk drawer and removed a heavy, silver-plated revolver, cocked it, put it to his temple, and pulled the trigger.

CHAPTER 4

She heard the voices and knew they were speaking to her, but they seemed far away, indistinct, a babble of nonsense words and terms that certainly had nothing to do with her.

"The suicide provision is quite clear," said one of the voices. "It is just about ironclad, I'm afraid."

There was a long, puzzled, embarrassed silence. Then someone shuffled papers. A throat cleared, a chair creaked.

"Can she hear us?"

"Is she all right?"

"Should I call a—"

"Mrs. Mott?"

Peyton Mott stirred. She was sitting stiffly at a conference table in the offices of the lawyers who had represented her husband for years. Arrayed before her at the table were the four partners. In the good times, when her husband had been one of the most prominent doctors in the city of Seattle, these same lawyers had been glad to handle his business. Now, in disgrace, they considered his wife and her problems an embarrassment, something to deal with quickly and quietly.

She was staring at them through clear, ice-blue eyes, her hands clasped in her lap. She was a strikingly beautiful woman, even in bereavement. Her alabaster skin and golden hair seemed to shine incandescently against the severe cut of her black Escada suit. Her startling blue eyes were wide-spaced and seemed to sparkle with innocence.

"I beg your pardon," she said.

The lawyer in charge of this painful session cleared his throat. "As I said, the suicide provision of the will is quite clear. However, we may be able to get the insurance company to return a small lump settlement."

"Small settlement?" said Peyton Mott.

Another lawyer took over. "As you know, Mrs. Mott, although your husband had sizable assets, they have been frozen by the state."

"Frozen?" There was no emotion on her face at all. It was as if she wasn't even in the room.

"Uh . . . this is normal procedure when it is probable that the estate will be sued by a number of sources." The lawyer broke off. Peyton's icy composure, her complete lack of emotion, was unnerving. For a moment he thought he would have preferred a grieving, wailing widow.

"Would you like a glass of water, Mrs. Mott?"

Very slowly she shook her head. "No, thank you."

"Of course, you are free to stay in the house until a sale comes through, but I do suggest that you begin to make some alternate plans for yourself."

"I see," she said. "Is that all?"

All of the lawyers looked at each other. No one had anything else to say and each of them was anxious to escape.

"That just about wraps things up for now, Mrs. Mott."

"Thank you," said Peyton. She rose, her back still perfectly straight. She took a few steps toward the door, then faltered. What little color she had drained from her cheeks. She put one hand out to steady herself on the edge of the table, the other dropping to the pronounced swell of her abdomen.

She whispered, "My baby . . ."

The lawyers were on their feet. "My God!"

Peyton's eyes rolled back in her head and she collapsed to the plushly carpeted floor.

The wail of the siren seemed to slice through her brain, rocketing her back to consciousness on a slick highway of pain. She was aware of a sharp stinging in her arm where the IV had been inserted.

But greater was the pain billowing up from between her legs. She managed to look down and saw bright red arterial blood coursing down her thighs, a paramedic working between her legs. Blood flecked his uniform shirt.

Peyton's eyes filled with fear and she screamed into the oxygen mask that was buckled firmly across her mouth and nose.

At the emergency room it was like being attacked. She was jolted out of the ambulance and onto a gurney, a team of trauma specialists falling on her bloody body like vultures. Her clothes were stripped from her and she was hastily wrapped in a paper hospital gown. Almost instantly the lower part of the garment was stained crimson.

As the gurney flew down the hall Peyton stared at the rapidly moving fluorescent light fixtures on the ceiling and heard a nurse shout, "She's going to need blood!"

"My baby," moaned Peyton. "Save my baby."

The table and the team blasted through the operating room doors and the doctors went to work. A variety of needles slid into her arm, drugs pulsing into her bloodstream. Doctors pounced on her, their hands probing and urgent. They were digging into her, cutting something out of her very core.

Her legs and thighs felt numb, but she sensed a wet and unnatural openness. Something pushed out of her and the doctors were no longer interested in her.

"He's out! Transfusion!"

He! It was a little boy! A boy to take the place of the man she had lost. "Please live," she moaned. *"Please . . ."*

"No heartbeat!"

"Fibrillate!"

There was a moment of silence, punctuated by the electronic hum and spit of medical machinery.

The voice was matter-of-fact, that of a seasoned professional with an easy familiarity with life and death. "Too late. Lost him."

Peyton lay in the hospital bed, unmoving beneath the sheets. Her lips were badly chapped and her blue eyes seemed to have sunk into her skull. She was scarcely aware of the nurse at her side or the tray of food spread before her. The nurse held a forkful in front of her mouth like a coaxing mother.

"You have *got* to eat," she said. "Don't you ever want to get out of here?"

Peyton did not answer. The nurse sighed in frustration.

"Three bites and then I'll leave you alone."

Peyton slowly shook her head on the pillow.

The nurse shook her head as well, then wearily gathered up the tray and utensils. "I'll be back with your breakfast. I am going to make *sure* you eat something on my shift!"

The words did not register on Peyton.

"You want to watch TV?" There was a TV bracketed to the wall facing the bed. The nurse snapped on the remote. "Watch some TV. Maybe you'll feel better."

The TV blathered on for an hour before Peyton's eyes flicked to the screen. The news had come on, but the first two or three items did not interest her. Then she heard some familiar words, some names she recognized.

". . . in a follow-up report to the case of Dr. Victor Mott, four civil suits, totaling fifteen million dollars, have been filed against the late doctor's estate. Although she was the first to accuse Mott of sexually molesting her during an examination, Mrs. Claire Bartel, of Madison Park, has not filed a suit. It was her accusation to the state medical board which led to the other women coming forward. . . ."

Peyton's eyes locked on the picture of Claire Bartel on the screen. She was being hustled out of a courthouse, surrounded by reporters and TV equipment. A man, presumably her husband, had his arm curved protectively around her shoulders. With the other he warded off the TV cameras and microphones. Peyton's eyes fastened on Claire's hands, which were clutched defensively across her stomach, as if shielding her unborn baby from the horrors of the world.

CHAPTER 5

Six months later

Joseph Bartel was born just after eight o'clock on a spring Sunday morning. He was a big baby, weighing eight pounds ten ounces, and he had the blue eyes of his father and the dark coloring of both of his parents. In the eyes of his parents, Claire and Michael, Joe was, without a doubt, the most beautiful baby boy in the entire history of the world. Claire gave birth without complications, and after a brief stay in the hospital, mother and son came home. Claire's world was complete.

Solomon had finished the fence many weeks earlier. During the time he worked on it, his position within the Bartel world had changed. He had lost his defensiveness, his timidity, relaxing in the loving atmosphere of the house. In a few short weeks Solomon had become almost a member of the Bartel family.

When the last slats of the elaborate fence were in place, Claire and Michael immediately found something else for him to do, setting him to painting the finely wrought trim of their Victorian house.

The family fell into a comfortable morning routine. Claire took the baby down early in the morning, placed him in his crib, and began breakfast, while Michael and Emma went through their morning Gilbert and Sullivan routine.

Solomon usually arrived at the backdoor of the house just as breakfast was done, performing a short peculiar ritual that never varied.

He would stand on the porch and announce, "I am approaching the backdoor."

Claire, working at the stove, smiled when she heard Solomon's deep, serious voice.

"I am now very near the backdoor."

Claire turned and waved. "Hi, Solomon."

Solomon opened the door, a smile on his face. "I am now coming through the backdoor."

"Help yourself to coffee."

Emma and Michael came thundering down

the stairs and burst into the kitchen, Emma bumping up against the crib. Little Joe, wriggling in his cot and alarmed by the sudden jolt, let out a startled wail.

"Oops. Sorry, Mom."

Instinctively Solomon reached into the bassinet to calm the baby.

Claire moved next to him and took the baby in her arms. "Solomon, remember the rule with the Better Day Society. It's best if you don't hold the baby."

Solomon's face crumpled. "I . . . I . . . I'm sorry," he stammered. "I forgot about the rule. I wanted to help."

"I know you did," she said evenly. "See, Joe's all right." She held the baby up for examination.

Solomon nodded earnestly, but he still looked a little shaken. "I'll take my coffee and finish outside," he mumbled.

"Solomon, you don't have to go outside."

"I know," he said with a smile. "But it's time to get to work."

Claire rocked the baby on her hip and turned to her husband. She had been formulating a plan for several days and now was as good a time as any to bring it up to Michael.

"They're replacing some of those smaller greenhouses down at the Botanical Gardens," she said casually. "I heard they're going to be giving away some of the frames."

Michael looked up from his breakfast and smiled slowly. "Let me guess—don't tell me. You want to build a greenhouse yourself."

Claire loved working in gardens and her volunteer work at the Seattle Botanical Gardens. She had always dreamed of starting a nursery, but she knew that such an undertaking was presently beyond her scope. However, she had been toying with the idea of starting a small business, perhaps raising fine herbs to supply to Seattle's growing number of gourmet food shops and good restaurants.

"Well," she said, hoping to convince her husband, "the hardware's already there. All I'd have to do is replace some of the glass, maybe do some leveling."

"Honey," said Michael seriously, "you're taking on an awful lot. Have you given any more thought to hiring a nanny?"

Claire shrugged. "Michael, I don't know about a nanny. It's so much money."

Michael frowned, knowing that there was more to her reluctance than money. He had recently been promoted and his salary had increased dramatically. There was no financial reason for not hiring a nanny and he knew it. "It's not the money, is it?"

"No," Claire admitted. "Not entirely. I've interviewed six girls so far and I wouldn't trust any of them with watering the plants, much less taking care of an infant."

"Well, you can't take care of everything yourself, Claire." Worry seemed to cross his face.

"What about Solomon?" suggested Emma. "*He* could be our nanny."

Claire and Michael exchanged a smile. "I don't know if he'd make such a good nanny, Emma."

"Why not?"

Claire chose her words carefully. Emma loved Solomon and would sit and talk to him for hours or, if she was lucky, coax him away from his work for a rough-and-tumble game of tag or a wrestling match. Claire figured that Emma realized that something about Solomon made him different from other people, but how much she understood, neither Michael nor Claire knew for sure. Claire did not want to make her daughter fear her new friend and knew she had to be diplomatic.

"Remember, we've talked about Solomon being mentally disabled?"

"Uh-huh," said Emma with a nod.

"Well, a disability like that makes him a very special person. So there are certain things that Solomon isn't able to do. Understand?"

Emma shook her head again. "Then what's going to happen when Solomon finishes his job painting the trim?"

"That's a good question." Emma and Claire immediately looked to Michael. Any decision to keep Solomon employed rested ultimately with him, and if he wanted to keep the women in his family happy, now was the time to make his move.

"Daddy?"

"Not to put any pressure on you, honey," said Claire sweetly.

"I guess we'll have to find something for him to do."

"Good!" shouted Emma.

"I'm glad that's settled," said Michael, "because I have to go to work."

Fifteen minutes after Michael left, Claire walked Emma to the school bus, holding the gate Solomon built open for her daughter. She could not look at the fence without smiling. It was a fine piece of work, perfectly level and artfully constructed, the pointed pickets standing up as straight as a line of soldiers.

Emma held back, as if unwilling to get on the bus. "Mom," she said in a very small voice, "I don't feel well."

Claire crouched down until her face was level

with her daughter's. "Go on to the bathroom and I'll hold the bus."

"It's not that. It's my head."

Claire laid her hand lightly on Emma's forehead. She had no fever, not even the hint of one. "Emma, is something worrying you about school today?"

Emma hesitated a moment, then the words came spilling out in a rush. "A mean kid at school has been picking on me."

Claire's brow knit in concern. "Did you tell your teacher about it?"

Eyes downcast, Emma nodded slowly.

Claire hugged her little girl. "Tell you what. I'll pick you up today and have a talk with him."

Emma looked at her mother, doubt in her eyes. "You're going to talk to him?" she said uncertainly.

"That's right? Is that okay?"

"I don't think you're mean enough. I wish Daddy would do it. Dad's a lot meaner than you are."

The school bus pulled up in front of the Bartel house and the doors swung open. Inside, Claire could hear the usual riot of third and fourth graders on their way to school.

"I promise I'll be mean. Don't worry, honey."

"I won't, Mom." Emma gave her mother a

quick kiss on the cheek and then clambered aboard the bus. Claire waved as it pulled away, then realized she was holding Emma's jacket.

"Wait!" She waved the garment in the air. "Emma! Stop! Your jacket!" She ran a few yards after the bus, but realized almost immediately that she couldn't catch it. It was moving down the hill, gathering speed, when abruptly it stopped. Claire sprinted to it and passed the jacket through the window.

A woman stepped from in front of the bus and waved at the driver. "Thanks. Thanks for stopping."

"No problem." The driver ground the gears and the bus moved off.

"Thank you," said Claire. "It's supposed to rain later and I forgot to give her the jacket."

"You're very welcome."

The two women hesitated awkwardly for a moment. "Well . . ." said Claire. "Thanks."

"I'm looking for the Bartel house," said the woman. "Would you happen to know where—"

"*I'm* Claire Bartel."

"Oh." The woman put out her hand. "My name is Peyton. Peyton Flanders. How do you do? I'm here about the nanny position."

"The nanny position?" said Claire, puzzled. "I don't recall the agency telling me about— you know, I completely forgot that I had scheduled you this morning. Usually I'm so good at keeping my appointments straight."

"I don't have an appointment," Peyton said quickly.

"You mean the agency just told you to stop by?"

"I'm not with an agency."

Claire shook her head as if to clear it. "I'm sorry, I don't understand."

Peyton's smile was disarming, almost vulnerable. "The truth is that I've only worked with one family and they're moving away. I wasn't sure what I was going to do next and then I was in the park with the little girl I take care of. . . ." Peyton shrugged. "Well, nannies talk, and I heard that your family was looking for someone. So—"

Claire had not been aware that the employment needs of her family were a topic of conversation in the city parks. It made her slightly uneasy. "I see."

Peyton shrugged again. "I'm sorry. I shouldn't have come. I can see that I've made you uncomfortable."

"No, no," said Claire quickly. "Don't go. You're here, so why don't you come up to the house."

Peyton's method may have been unorthodox, but Claire could see that she was more the kind of woman she wanted for her children's nanny than the ones she had interviewed. She was older and seemed more steady, solid. Peyton was also neatly dressed in an expensive black raincoat, pleated gray wool slacks, a modest white blouse, and a striking purple silk scarf.

It didn't take Claire long to make a pot of tea and the two women settled at the coffee table in the family room. Peyton's eyes scanned the room, taking in the family photographs, the old but well-cared-for Mission furniture, the simple watercolors on the walls, the luxuriant green of the plants. Hooked to the back of Claire's chair was a small loudspeaker, a device not much bigger than a cigarette pack, a portable intercom. These were the details of Claire Bartel's life and Peyton memorized them, drinking them in.

"I usually have a whole set of prepared questions," said Claire with a rueful smile. "They usually begin with 'Have you finished high school?' and 'Are you old enough to drive?' But I can see that in your case—"

"Am I too old?" asked Peyton, a look of alarm in her eyes.

"No, not at all. Quite the contrary."

Peyton seemed to relax a little. "That's a relief."

Just then one of Claire's faux diamond earrings fell to the floor, like a tear. Peyton bent to retrieve it.

"Don't lose this," she said.

Claire clipped the earring back in place. "The backing is loose. My husband has been after me to get it fixed. There just never seems to be enough time."

"I'll bet with two children it seems like there aren't ever enough hours in the day."

Claire nodded. "That's why we're looking for a nanny. How did you happen to become one yourself?"

For a moment Peyton looked troubled, as if the shadow of an old memory had crossed her beautiful face. Her voice grew solemn and sad. "A few years ago I went through a difficult time in my life. . . . I lost my husband and my baby within a few days of one another." It looked as if a tear would spill down her pale cheek.

"I'm sorry," said Claire. She shifted in her chair, uncomfortable that a complete stranger was sharing such deep confidences.

"The miscarriage prevented me from ever having another child," Peyton said sadly, then took a deep breath. "A mutual friend set me up with a family that was looking for a nanny. It turned out to be wonderful."

Claire cleared her throat. Briefly she imagined herself in the same terrible position, feeling ashamed at the thought of what her own emotional response would have been. "Forgive me for asking, but you didn't feel any . . . jealousy?"

Peyton smiled brightly. It was like the sun coming out from behind a cloud. "Oh, no. I adore children, Mrs. Bartel. And I take the job of raising them very seriously. For me the work is incredibly rewarding. It's the next best thing to being a mother."

"That's so refreshing to hear," said Claire. She was relieved that Peyton's bleak mood had passed, leaving not a trace of self-pity behind. "I'm starting an herb business in the backyard, something quite small, but it will be keeping me very busy and I'll have less time for the children, even though I'll be working at home. So I'm looking for someone who can help me fill in the gaps around here."

"Your own business," said Peyton admiringly. "How wonderful."

"It's something I've dreamed of doing for a long time now."

"You seem to have everything you could possibly want," said Peyton evenly. "Perfect."

"I'm lucky," Claire admitted.

From the intercom speaker came the happy, contented gurgle of baby Joe. He was in his room upstairs and was just waking up from his nap.

Claire jumped up. "That's my boy," she said with a little laugh. "Right on time and hungry as a bear, I'll bet."

"I'd love to meet him," said Peyton softly.

Claire led Peyton up the stairs to the second story of the house. "The nursery's right next to our bedroom, and with the intercom we can hear everything he—"

"Claire! Are you up there?" Solomon was standing in the well of the staircase. "I want to check the color of the trim with you."

"Up here, Solomon."

Solomon climbed the stairs and stopped outside the baby's room. He looked shyly at Peyton. First encounters with strangers were always difficult for him and Peyton's blue eyes were scanning him intently, wide and knowing, as if reading him in an instant.

"Solomon," said Claire. "Meet Peyton. Solomon is painting the trim."

"Nice to meet you, Solomon."

"Hello," said Solomon timorously. Awkwardly he shook her hand, the paint on his fingers staining the cuff of her linen blouse. Peyton pulled back her hand as if she had been scalded and rubbed at the spot.

"Oh! I'm sorry!" Solomon cringed as if he expected her to hit him.

Peyton struggled to keep her anger under control. Her smile was tight and false. "That's quite all right. It was an accident. Anyone can have an accident."

Joe cried out. "It's time for lunch," said Claire.

"I'll get back to work," mumbled Solomon.

Claire took Joe from the crib and held him in front of her for a moment. Every time she saw her son, she felt him take her breath away. This perfect little person was hers, her creation, her abiding, immutable joy.

"He's beautiful," said Peyton softly. She looked curiously around the room. It was light and airy, wallpapered in bright colors, with a crib, a changing table, and a chest of drawers. A marble fireplace was set into one wall, with a pair of andirons and a set of fire irons—poker, tongs, and shovel—in a rack.

Sitting in the white rocking chair—Emma's old rocker—in the corner of the nursery, Claire couldn't restrain herself from flashing Peyton the smile of proud motherhood. When she slipped her breast out of her feeding bra, Joe clutched at it, his mouth fastening on the swollen nipple, a little hand laid against the curve of her chest, as if to hold his mother close.

It was a timeless scene, mother and infant, Madonna and child, a picture of calm and ageless serenity. Peyton burned with jealousy.

"Look at the time," she said, fighting to hold down the envy and resentment in her voice. "I've taken up half your morning." She had to get out of there before she screamed in anger and covetousness. "I can show myself out."

She pulled an envelope from her purse. "These are my references. I'll leave them on the hall table."

Claire felt warm and fulfilled, at peace with the world, as if the baby at her breast were all she could ask for in life. "Peyton," she said impulsively, "are you free for dinner tonight? I'd love you to meet my husband and Emma."

Peyton paused at the door and thought for a moment. A second or two before she had been on the verge of abandoning her plan, but suddenly revenge forced itself back into her soul, flooding her veins with a mad intoxicant.

"Tonight? I'd love to."

CHAPTER 6

Exactly why Roth had taken such a dislike to her, Emma Bartel could not say. Roth was a boy a little older than she, a little bigger than most of the children in the playground of the Denny-Blaine School. He was nasty and bullying with most of the children, but he saved his most malicious taunts and tricks for Emma.

He was a skilled little bully, too, careful never to allow his torments to be observed by the parents of his victims or the teachers at the school. But in the playground he maintained a tiny-tot reign of terror. Emma had always enjoyed going to school, but as Roth's harassment grew in severity she became more and more reluctant to attend. When she was in class, under the protection of her teacher, Mrs. Henry, she felt secure. It was when the bell rang that she felt that sinking feeling, the sense of childhood doom.

True to her word, Claire Bartel arrived to pick up her daughter from school and to have a word with Emma's teacher about the little boy who was making her child miserable. Adults, though, who take their own likes and dislikes very seriously, never quite understand just how important the same elements are in the lives of their children, no matter how young they might be.

It was, Mrs. Henry and Claire decided, nothing more than a misunderstanding that could be mended with a simple handshake, or the five-year-old equivalent.

The teacher and Claire stood over Roth and Emma and tried to effect a reconciliation.

"Now, Emma," said Mrs. Henry evenly, "has Roth been bothering you?"

Roth, a head taller than Emma, kept his cool. He looked straight at his victim as if daring her to rat on him. Emma looked hopelessly at her mother. Couldn't she *see* what he was conveying wordlessly?

"Darling," said Claire, "you can tell Mrs. Henry."

Children have a finely developed sense of

honor, a code of playground honor as rigorous as anything developed by criminals.

"No," she said. "He doesn't bother me."

Roth folded his arms and smirked at the adults, like a crime boss who has beaten the rap.

"Roth," said Claire, "maybe you and Emma could be friends. Do you think you could?"

"Oh, yeah," said Roth. "Sure."

"See, Emma," said Mrs. Henry smoothly. "There's nothing to be afraid of."

Emma took her mother by the hand. "Let's go, Mom."

"Say good-bye to Mrs. Henry and Roth," advised Claire.

"Good-bye," said Emma. Roth was standing just behind the teacher.

"Bye, Emma," he said brightly. Then he raised his fist and silently mouthed the words "dead meat."

Emma took to Peyton immediately, insisting on taking her by the hand and showing the nanny all of her favorite places in the house. She guided Peyton to her bedroom and solemnly introduced her by name to each of her stuffed toys and dolls. It was with some difficulty that Claire coaxed them into the kitchen, insisting that Emma assist her in preparing dinner. She put a whisk in her daughter's hand and set her to mixing the salad dressing.

As Claire moved from stove to refrigerator to cookbook Peyton toyed with Joe, who gurgled happily in his bassinet.

"Why don't you have a family of your own?" asked Emma.

"Emma, don't ask rude questions," Claire cautioned.

"That's okay," said Peyton. "It's because being a nanny, I get to join in another family."

This explanation seemed to satisfy Emma. She returned to whisking the dressing.

"We're very glad to have Peyton with us, aren't we, Emma?" said Claire. She was frowning down at her cookbook.

"Yes," said Emma matter-of-factly. "I'm in charge of stirring the salad dressing, Peyton."

"I can see that."

"And now you're in charge of setting the table," ordered Claire. "Daddy will be home any minute."

"Okay." Emma nodded, gathered up the knives and forks, and started laying four places on the table.

"If you don't mind me asking," said Peyton, "what does Mr. Bartel do for a living?"

"Daddy's a mad scientist," said Emma.

Claire and Peyton exchanged smiles.

"Not quite," said Claire. "Michael's a genetic engineer. He works for an outfit called Biotechniques. Right now he's developing a bacteria that would protect crops from frost."

"It's called ice-minus," said Emma knowingly.

"Michael's trying to pass it through the Environmental Protection Agency. It's the last step in a three-year project. They get real touchy about letting strange new bacteria out into the world." More immediate concerns took Claire's mind off her husband's project. "Emma, put down the place mats first."

But Emma had lost interest in her job. The front door slammed. "It's Daddy!" she shouted happily.

She ran into her father's arms. He lifted her and hugged her.

"Hello, monkey face."

"I am not!" Emma insisted gleefully.

He crossed to his wife and kissed her lovingly. "Hello, sweetheart." Over Claire's shoulder he caught sight of Peyton. He pulled away from the embrace, slightly embarrassed.

"Michael," said Claire. "I want you to meet Peyton."

"Hello," said Peyton, taking his hand in hers. She held it for a fraction of a second longer than normal and looked him square in the eye.

"Very nice to meet you, Peyton." Their eyes locked for a split second.

"Daddy! You have to hurry! Dinner is almost ready! Go wash up the way you're supposed to!" Emma was pulling her father toward the door.

"My goodness, we are bossy tonight."

By the end of dinner that night Peyton had settled into the Bartel family. She was light and gracious at supper, always ready to assist Claire in serving and clearing, but never asserting herself, never forgetting her secondary position in the family.

Claire managed to get Michael alone in the kitchen for a moment. "What do you think?" she asked, whispering so Peyton could not hear them.

"She's terrific," Michael murmured back. "What's the catch?"

"There's no catch. She won't be a nanny forever, but I think we can get her to commit to a year."

"That sounds great. Let's grab her before she gets a better offer."

Peyton was still sitting at the dining-room table. Emma walked back and forth between the kitchen and dining room, ferrying plates.

Joe cooed and bubbled in his bassinet next to Peyton.

"When Mom finishes the greenhouse, I'll be in charge of the strawberries," Emma said.

"Is that so? That sounds like a very important job." Peyton was only half listening to the little girl. She spotted Claire's earring, the one with the loose clip, lying on the floor. She knelt quickly and picked it up.

"It is," said Emma. "Mom says that strawberries need a lot of care."

"I'll bet." Peyton watched the little girl walk back into the kitchen.

Then she stood and thrust the earring into Joe's mouth and swung into her act. "Joe!"

The Bartels heard her voice, alarmed and excited. Claire bolted back into the dining room, Michael and Emma right behind her.

Peyton was leaning into the bassinet. "Joe!" She thrust her fingers into his soft little mouth.

Michael and Claire crowded around the bassinet. "What is it?"

"He had something in his mouth," said Peyton. "He was about to swallow this." She held out her hand. Glistening in her palm was something shiny and hard.

"Mommy's earring!" shouted Emma.

Claire's hand went to her ear. She looked horror-struck. "He must have grabbed it off my ear when I burped him." She looked guiltily at her husband. "I'm sorry."

"It's okay," said Michael. "Joe's fine."

"I'm sorry I frightened everybody," said Peyton quietly.

"No, no," said Michael. "I'm glad you caught it."

Claire lifted Joe out of his crib and held him close. He cooed, delighted to be in her arms.

"Thank God Peyton got there in time," said Michael.

CHAPTER 7

Peyton returned to the Bartel home the next morning. Carrying a suitcase and shopping bag, she mounted the porch steps and then paused before the front door, her hand in midair. She sensed, eerily, that she was being watched. Slowly she turned and looked up.

Solomon was high on a ladder, under the eaves of the house, a piece of sandpaper in his hand. He was staring down at her, suddenly fearful.

Peyton looked at him for a moment, her eyes emotionless. Then she forced a wide, feigned smile and waved. Timidly he waved back and then returned to his task.

Claire answered the door. "We'll have to see about getting you a set of keys," she said.

"I brought a present," said Peyton, proffering the shopping bag. "It's something for Joe."

"You really didn't have to." Claire burrowed into the folds of tissue paper and pulled out a set of wind chimes. The tubes of the bells jangled and jingled against each other, a haunting hollow sound.

"They say a wind chime helps a baby sleep," said Peyton.

"I love it! I'll tell you what; let's get you settled downstairs and then we'll hang it outside the nursery window."

"Great."

Peyton's room was in the basement beyond the furnace room and the laundry. The cellar stairs were steep and dark and the utility rooms dark and shadowy, the walls roughly finished. Wiring snaked along the tops of the partitions and the furnace roared dully in the background. Claire suddenly felt embarrassed at consigning Peyton to the basement, as if it somehow denigrated her.

"This part feels a little dark," she said defensively, "but your room gets plenty of light." She pushed into the bedroom.

Michael and Claire had done their best to make the room comfortable and welcoming.

There was a large bed with a bright spread and several pieces of light wicker furniture. A new television set stood on a stand in the corner and an elaborate digital clock radio was on the night table.

"I hope it's okay," said Claire.

Peyton's smile was wide and winning. "It's perfect...."

The last thing Claire did before going to bed was look in on her son. She would stand over the crib watching his easy and tranquil sleep, his little chest rising and falling. She gazed at him, enraptured, for a long time until her own exhaustion began to overcome her. She kissed Joe's satiny cheek, checked that the intercom on the changing table was working, and then went to her own room.

Michael was already in bed, a yellow legal pad propped up on his knees. He frowned at the pages, covered with hundreds of complex equations and calculations, as he worked and re-worked the figures.

Claire came out of the bathroom dressed in a silken, short nightgown, pulling a single spaghetti strap down from her slim shoulders. She leaned against the door frame.

"Opportunity knocks," she said with a smile.

Michael grinned sheepishly. "Angel, you know this EPA proposal is due next week."

Claire walked to the bed and slipped in between the sheets, snuggling against her husband, kissing his neck and ear.

"It's not fair to take advantage of a weak man, especially in the middle of the equation."

"How much time you need?"

Michael glanced at the clock. "Can you hold on until eleven-thirty?"

Claire rubbed herself against her husband, like a cat demanding attention. "We could throw caution to the wind and do it at eleven-seventeen."

"Eleven-thirty," Michael insisted.

"You got yourself a date," said Claire. She curled in the bed, her head deep in the soft pillow.

Michael turned back to his numbers, deep in thought. But it didn't take long for the digits to start swimming before his eyes. He rubbed them vigorously and tried to focus again, but weariness was overtaking him.

He put down his work and snapped off the bedside light. He nestled against his wife, his hands traveling under her filmy negligee, massaging her smooth, cool body. Claire groaned and almost awoke. But she remained asleep and soon her exhausted husband joined her.

Deep in the night, the digital alarm clock next to Peyton's bed snapped on, a low humming buzz. She was awake instantly, her hand shooting out to turn it off.

She slipped out of bed like a snake and stood for a moment in the middle of her dark room, her head cocked, listening to the noises of the old house. She was dressed in a light, cotton nightdress, its only touch of ornament a little lace at the collar and cuffs. Her feet were bare.

Very cautiously, like an intruder, she climbed the basement stairs, crossed the living room, and mounted the steps to the second floor.

On the landing outside the bedrooms she paused again, like an animal sniffing the wind. She listened so intently that it seemed as if she wasn't listening at all, but staring at some fixed point in the darkness. Then, very carefully, as if defusing a bomb or cracking a safe, she turned the doorknob of the nursery, entering the room and closing the door behind her.

She paused again for a moment, absorbing the smell of the room, the clean fragrance of baby, powder, and soap. Eyes wide to catch the little light in the room, Peyton crossed the room, picked up a baby pillow from the rocking chair, and approached the crib. She held the pillow out in front of her like a weapon. For a moment she held the pillow over Joe's silent, still face, as if unsure of what to do next. Then she walked away and carefully placed the pillow over the intercom on the changing table, muffling it.

Peyton lifted Joe from the crib, murmuring in his ear, waking him gently, quieting his cranky cries. She carried the baby to the rocking chair and sat down, cradling him in her arms.

She slipped her breast out of the nightgown and placed her nipple in his hungry mouth. Joe eagerly sucked and suckled, nestling against her soft skin. Her milk flowed from her like a warm stream and she felt a luscious electricity pulse through her, relief and pleasure blazing from her face.

"Oh, baby," she breathed.

Moonlight streamed through the windows. Outside the wind chimes gently swayed and tinkled in the wind.

CHAPTER 8

The days moved with an easy rhythm, a settled routine that comforted the Bartels and Solomon and filled Peyton with a sense of impending triumph. Like a burr she had worked her way into the Bartels' life, effortlessly burrowing into the flesh of the family like a dormant disease.

Michael, Claire, and Emma extended their trust to her, unaware of what they were harboring in their midst. Peyton had made herself essential to the smooth running of the household.

Although hired as a nanny, Peyton quickly took over other tasks. The greenhouse was being built in the backyard, and when Claire was not there to oversee its construction, Peyton kept an eye on the workmen. She ran errands, did the shopping, cooked, and cleaned.

But she was not a servant. It did not take long for Peyton to become a pal and confidante to Emma and a friend to Claire. She was always ready with a helping hand and a smile, a calming word to Emma, and good solid advice for Claire. There was a slight inequality between the women, a lingering difference in status, but this was as things should have been.

The only coldness in the family existed between Solomon and Peyton. They circled each other warily, like wrestlers looking for a hold. Only their individual motives varied. All Solomon wanted was to steer clear of Peyton. She knew, sensed, that a confrontation was coming and that when the time came, she would have to drive him from the house. She had no doubt that she could do this with ease.

On some occasions Peyton's position shifted slightly but significantly. The pull and stress of Claire and Michael's busy days didn't allow much time for recreation or socializing, but from time to time their friends managed to get them to agree to an evening out.

At such times Peyton was promoted, as it were, becoming a sort of younger sister helping her older sibling get ready for a big date.

Fresh from bathing and wrapped in a towel, Claire sat at the vanity in the bedroom dabbing perfume oil on her warm neck and in the soft valley between her breasts. Peyton stood behind her, watching her every move, like a kid who dreams of one day doing the same thing.

"I don't think it'll be a late night," said Claire. She looped a gold bracelet around her wrist, red stones shimmering for a moment in the mirror. "We're having dinner at the Union Square Grill. I'll write down the number for you."

Peyton nodded. She knew the restaurant well. It was, perhaps, the most expensive and most chic restaurant in Seattle. In the old days she and her husband had dined there frequently, and the owner of the place used to escort them to their usual table personally.

"Fine, fine," she said dutifully. "Claire, that's a beautiful bracelet. Rubies?"

Claire held her arm out and admired the bracelet. "No, not rubies. I wish. They're garnets. Michael got it for me at an antiques fair."

Peyton had had to sell most of her jewelry after her husband's death. She looked covetously at the finely wrought piece.

"You can borrow it anytime you like," said Claire.

"Thank you." Peyton turned from the mirror

to admire the dress that lay on the bed. It was shiny red silk, and seemed to sparkle; it was obvious that it would set off Claire's dark coloring to distinct advantage.

"Wow," Peyton said admiringly. "This must be a special occasion."

"I always feel completely glamorous and sexy when I wear this dress. It was a present from Michael, too. It's his favorite."

"I can see why," said Peyton with a knowing smile and a little wink.

"Better put on my stockings first." Claire stepped into her walk-in closet and started rummaging in a drawer. Peyton picked up the bottle of perfume oil as if merely toying with it.

"Which way should I go with the stockings?" called Claire. "Black or nude?"

Peyton opened the bottle of scent. "What color are the shoes?" Deftly she smeared a spot of the heavy oil on the collar of the dress. The liquid seeped into the silk, leaving an ugly and obvious stain.

"Black," called Claire from the closet.

"Then definitely go with black hose." Peyton put the perfume back on the vanity table. This little act of sabotage was exhilarating. She had to suppress an evil little smirk.

Claire returned wearing the black stockings.

She picked up the dress and put it on, the filmy material slithering sensuously over her body.

"Thank you for helping me with these earth-shattering decisions." She turned her bare back to Peyton. "Would you mind zipping me up?"

A car horn sounded in the street in front of the Bartel house.

"That's them," said Claire. "I'd better hurry."

"Have fun," said Peyton.

Claire gave herself a last look in the mirror, leaning forward and squinting. "Damn!"

"What? What is it?"

"There's a stain on this dress. It just came back from the cleaners. I can't believe it." She sniffed at the blotch. There was another impatient honk from the street.

"It's my perfume. I must have had the perfume oil on my hands."

"Don't move. I'll get some club soda." Peyton dashed from the room and down the stairs.

Michael and another man were standing in the foyer. Marty Craven was a little taller than Michael, a little more handsome, a little richer, and a little better dressed. He and his wife, Marlene, were old friends of the Bartels and they lived in a larger, more luxurious home just a few doors down the street.

"What's keeping you guys?"

"Running late," said Michael apologetically. "Does Marlene want to come inside?"

"Nah," said Marty. "She's on the phone." Marlene was a prominent real-estate agent and she never wasted a moment. The bills on her car phone were astronomical. Marty looked up the stairs and caught sight of Peyton.

"Marty, this is Peyton."

"Well, hello, Peyton," Marty said with a big grin. His eyes swept over her and he made no attempt to hide the fact that he approved of what he saw.

"Nice to meet you. Please excuse me." She moved on to the kitchen.

Marty winked at Michael. "Maybe we should go ahead and have kids."

"Just wanted to inform everyone," said a voice behind him, "that this place will not—I repeat, not—hold our table." Marlene Craven, Marty's wife, stood in the doorway.

"Marlene," said Michael, "you look beautiful." He kissed her lightly on the cheek.

He was telling the truth. Marlene was a thin, slinky woman in her thirties with fine features and perfectly cut auburn hair. Her clothes were very expensive and up-to-the-moment stylish. But there was a hardness about her brown eyes, which took in all and analyzed it according to her personal standards.

At the moment they regarded her husband suspiciously. "What's with you?"

"What do you mean, what's with me? Nothing's with me." Marty shifted nervously. Even when he *hadn't* done anything wrong, Marlene had this way of making him feel guilty.

Peyton emerged from the kitchen, a bottle of club soda in her hand. Marlene nodded to herself, as if something had been confirmed.

Marlene took Peyton in at a glance. "Nothing, my ass." The smile on her lips didn't extend to her eyes. "I don't believe we've met." She extended a thin hand with blood-red nails. "I'm Marlene Craven. You must be Peyton."

Peyton knew an enemy when she saw one. "Hello." She tried to brush by, but Marlene blocked her path.

"Poison," she said.

"Pardon?"

"The perfume. You're wearing Claire's perfume. Poison. Christian Dior."

"Please excuse me," said Peyton demurely. "Claire needs me upstairs."

Marty's eyes followed Peyton up the staircase.

"What," asked Marlene acidly, "are you looking at?"

Claire had changed her clothes quickly, but she was not pleased with her appearance. In place of the gold dress, she now wore a long, floral-patterned Laura Ashley, a high lace color at her throat. She was disappointed, having metamorphosed from sexy to respectable. Not a matron exactly, but definitely a mother.

"I brought the club soda," said Peyton.

"It's too late," said Claire. "Another time."

"You look terrific."

Claire appeared at the top of the stairs and looked down. Marlene and Michael were arm in arm and she was flirting effortlessly with him. Her face dropped as she saw Marlene's perfect outfit. She felt dowdy and drab. She felt the faint sizzle of jealousy in her blood.

"Sorry to hold everyone up," she said, coming down the stairs.

"Here she is," said Marlene. "Looking gorgeous as usual." She kissed and embraced Claire with a genuine affection. "Would someone please look at this beautiful kid?"

"I thought you were going to wear that sexy silk number," said Michael.

Irritation flashed across Claire's face. "Is there something wrong with what I'm wearing?"

Michael stammered, trying to dig himself out of the mess he suddenly found himself in. "I didn't mean—I think you look *great*, honey. I—"

Marlene took Claire by the arm and ushered her out the door. She shot a dirty look at Michael.

"What you don't know about women is a lot," she said with a smirk.

"Have fun," Peyton called brightly.

CHAPTER 9

Peyton shifted roles effortlessly. In the space of a few minutes she went from kid sister to Claire to big sister to Emma. When the grown-ups went out the front door, she and Emma giggled together, clapping their hands, heady with the prospect of having the run of the house. Peyton whipped up a batch of popcorn, dripping with butter and salt, and allowed Emma as many sodas as she could possibly drink.

They carried their goodies down to Peyton's room like kids hiding themselves in their secret lair. They wallowed in a couple of hours of unrestricted TV watching, the more mindless the better, finishing up with a great big chunk of horror movies on the late-night creature-feature show. Emma was in seventh heaven.

"This is great!" she exclaimed. "Mom *never* lets me watch this show."

Peyton winked. "That's why we have to keep it a secret."

Emma's eyes grew wide. "A secret?"

"Do you know what a secret is?" Peyton whispered conspiratorially.

Emma nodded. "Yes. It's something you can't tell anybody, no matter what."

"That's right. And now we have our own secret club."

"We *do*?" Emma sounded thrilled at the thought of having a secret club with a grown-up. She was sure that no one else in her class could make that claim.

"That's right. It's a special club for just the two of us."

"Wow!" Emma snuggled in Peyton's arms. "I've never been in a secret club before."

"Well, just remember . . ."

"I know. It's a secret." Emma crammed a small fistful of popcorn into her mouth.

Peyton knew that children almost always told the truth and that Emma would be a valuable source of information on the intimacies of the Bartel family.

"You know," she said casually, "it was lots of

fun meeting your aunt Marlene and uncle Marty. Don't you think they're real nice?"

"Yes." Emma nodded. "They give me nice presents every year. On my birthday and at Christmas."

"They do? Have they always done that? Ever since you were little?"

"Since even before I was born."

"So they must have known your mommy and daddy for a very long time."

Emma smiled slightly, as if she was about to make her first contribution to the secret club. "Aunt Marlene grew up with Daddy. They used to be boyfriend and girlfriend."

Peyton smirked. Jackpot! This was information she could use to good effect. "Is that so?"

"Uh-huh." Emma's eyes strayed to the TV set.

Peyton wanted to keep the conversation going. She smoothed the little girl's hair. "Do you have any boyfriends?"

Emma sat bolt upright and grimaced. "Yilch! No! I hate boys."

"Hate boys? How come?"

"If I tell you something, you promise not to tell anyone?" Emma whispered.

"Promise," said Peyton seriously. "Secret club, remember?"

"There's this boy at school; his name is Roth

and he's been really really mean to me, but he said if I told on him, I'd be dead meat."

"He *said* that?"

Emma nodded. "Peyton, he's *so* mean to me."

"What does he do?"

"Mean stuff."

"Like what?" Peyton persisted.

Emma thought for a moment. "Well, this one time he came up to me on the playground and he told me he had a bee."

"A bee?"

"Yeah, with a stinger. And he put it on my head and told me that I shouldn't move, otherwise the bee would sting me."

"And what did you do?"

"I stood still. I didn't move. But then the bell rang and all the other kids went back into class and I was afraid to move, so I didn't. So Mrs. Henry came out looking for me and I wouldn't tell on Roth and she got mad at me." Emma sniffled a little at the painful memory and she burrowed deeper into Peyton's arms.

"I can't believe it. What was it he called you?"

"Dead meat," said Emma.

"That's terrible. Why didn't you tell your mommy?"

"I *did*, but it didn't do any good. I don't think

she believed me. I think she thought I was making it all up and I wasn't."

"*I* believe you," said Peyton stoutly. "And *I'll* fix Roth for you. But *good*."

"You will?"

"You bet."

"That would be great!"

"Leave it to me."

Peyton hugged Emma tightly, quivering with anger at the thought of the cruelty children inflicted on other children.

After the rocky start, dinner at the Union Square Grill had settled down. The food had been excellent and the bottle of wine the four adults shared had taken the edge off the evening. Conversation was determined by gender—Claire and Marlene talking quietly on their side of the table, Marty and Michael deep in discussion on theirs.

Marlene lighted her cigarette with an expensive lighter, a heavy hunk of gold. Claire didn't like smoking, but it was the price you had to pay if you wanted Marlene's friendship.

Claire picked up the lighter and hefted it in her hand. "This is a beauty," she said. "It's almost worth smoking to have a thing like that."

Marlene tapped her ash emphatically. "It's

Tiffany," she said. "Marty got it on his last trip to New York." She tossed her lighter aside and fixed a determined look at Claire. "I have to tell you something," she said.

Claire smiled. Marlene *always* had something to tell somebody. It was another price you paid.

"I want to talk to you about that nanny of yours."

"Peyton? What's the problem?"

"She's the problem."

"No, she isn't. She's been wonderful. Emma loves her and she treats Joe as if he were her own. Frankly I feel lucky to have her. If you could have met some of the airheads I interviewed before she came along, you would understand what I mean."

Marlene looked unconvinced. "I'm warning you—she could be trouble."

"Trouble?" Claire laughed. "What kind of trouble could Peyton possibly cause?"

"You never, *never*, let an attractive woman take a power position in your home, Claire. It's a bad business. It's as simple as that."

"Peyton?" said Claire. "Power position?"

Marlene nodded shortly and drew on her cigarette. "You heard me," she said, exhaling a cloud of blue-gray smoke. "What's that saying? The hand with the baby . . . the cradle that rocks . . ."

Marty leaned into their conversation. "Hey, Marlene, how much did you get for the Fletcher house last week?"

The calculator built into Marlene's head clicked. "Three and change." She turned back to Claire. "All I'm saying is that you have to watch your back."

Claire rolled her eyes. "C'mon. . . ." But she felt for Michael's hand under the table and squeezed it.

"I'm serious," Marlene insisted. "It's a war out there, Claire, and you can't afford a battle on your home front. There's too much pressure. These days a woman is a failure if she doesn't bring in fifty grand a year and still make time for sex and homemade lasagna—"

Michael butted into the conversation. "What on earth are you two talking about?"

"Combat," said Claire with a laugh.

"Marlene's not much of a cook, but she sure gives great lasagna." Marty cackled at his own joke.

"Add two children to the mix and you need to hire help, Marlene," said Claire matter-of-factly. "The superwoman stuff wears thin after a while."

Michael shot a guilty glance at his wife, then slipped a cigarette out of Marlene's pack. "I'm going to bum one of these, Marlene, if you don't mind."

"Help yourself."

"You're a horrible influence," said Claire. "He never smokes anymore except with you."

Michael took a deep drag, savoring the smoke. "Once in a while isn't going to kill me."

"It makes you smell like an ashtray."

Marlene wasn't really listening; she was busy trying to think of something. Suddenly she clutched Claire's forearm. "Got it. The hand that rocks the cradle," she said, "is the hand that rules the world."

CHAPTER 10

Peyton's days followed a set routine. By mid-morning she had finished putting the Bartel house in order and had seen Claire off to her volunteer work at the Seattle Botanical Gardens. Before lunch she was heading for the park, pushing Joe in his baby carriage.

It was her favorite part of the day, out among the young mothers and their babies, in the sun and fresh air. She always lost herself in the same fantasy, that Joe was hers, that she had a family and home as perfect as the Bartels'. Well, it would all come to her in the end. She knew it. She deserved it. It was her destiny.

Peyton settled herself on a park bench and checked on Joe. He was awake and staring wide-eyed at the great world around him. She chucked him under the chin and cooed at him, being rewarded with a heart-melting smile.

"Boy or girl?" someone asked.

Peyton looked up. A woman was standing over the carriage. She was a little older than Peyton, and she, too, had a baby. Peyton couldn't help but notice that the woman's baby wasn't nearly as good-looking as her little Joe.

"Boy," she said with a sweet, engaging smile. "His name is Joe." She took the baby out of the stroller and rested him on her hip proudly, as if a baby were a badge of office.

"Hello, Joe," said the woman.

Joe gurgled and wriggled and smiled.

How many months?"

"Three," said Peyton.

"He's beautiful. He has your eyes, you know."

Peyton beamed. "You really think so?"

The two women chatted for a few minutes, the way young mothers do, each drawing from the collective experiences of childbearing and rearing. Peyton made the obligatory fuss over the woman's little girl, praising her looks and smile, and watched as her new acquaintance swelled with pride.

When the woman showed signs of getting a little friendlier, Peyton put her off gently, remembering an appointment she had almost forgotten. . . .

Emma, her legs pumping, pushed the swing as high as she could, enjoying the rush of wind through her hair and the warmth of the sun on her face. Recess was half over, and so far so good—Roth had not spoken to her, but he shot a glance in her direction from time to time, as if waiting for the right moment to launch an attack. He was in a sandbox, holding forth to his circle of cowed cronies. Emma feared the worst.

Suddenly her swing stopped in midarc. Peyton stood behind her, holding the seat.

"Hi, Peyton."

"Hi, honey." Peyton gave Emma a peck on the cheek and whispered in her ear. "Which one is he?"

Emma pointed.

"Got it." The nanny released the swing and marched across the schoolyard.

Roth was bragging. "So I said, no problemo, amigo. You're history. *Bam!*" He slammed a fist into a palm. His courtiers giggled nervously. "That's what happens when you mess with me. *Bam!*" He struck his hands together again and waited for the laughter.

But it didn't come.

The three boys were looking up at Peyton, who towered over them like a statue. Before Roth could react, she reached down and yanked him to his feet.

"Ow," he squealed. "My arm!"

Peyton hauled him up until the toes of his sneakers were brushing the sand, his face close to hers. "I have a message for you, Roth," she growled, her voice low and throaty. "Leave Emma alone, Roth. If you continue to mess with her, I'm going to rip your head off. Am I clear?"

Huge tears began running down Roth's face. Peyton shook him like a terrier with a rat. "I said, is that clear?"

Roth couldn't speak through his tears. He blubbered and nodded his head vigorously. "Good," Peyton snarled. She let go of the boy's arm and he toppled to the ground in a whimpering heap. Every child in the playground was watching this little scene in stunned fascination.

Their eyes followed Peyton as she marched triumphantly across the schoolyard. As she passed Emma she gave her a wink. "Secret club," she whispered.

The little girl on the swing next to Emma looked approvingly at Peyton as she wheeled Joe away. "Your mom is *so* cool."

"She's not my mom," Emma said quietly.

"I wish my mom was cool like that."

Emma stared after Peyton. She did have to admit that Peyton *was* pretty cool. And there was no denying that she had succeeded where her own mother had failed miserably. She felt happy and grateful, delighted that she wouldn't have to put up with Roth's torments anymore. And it was all due to Peyton. Why hadn't her own mother done it so quickly, with so little fuss? The difference between these two women was a mystery to her. Her mom was a mom. Peyton was more like a friend.

Emma looked over at her former enemy and felt a little sorry for him.

Roth continued to sob in the sandbox and the children looked at him with the contempt they reserve for fallen tyrants. They were all glad that Peyton had appeared out of nowhere and handled Roth so easily. Each and every one of them was well aware that Roth's day of glory was past.

CHAPTER 11

The early mornings had always been special for Claire. In those quiet hours before the house, the world, came alive, before the day became clouded with the petty irritations of daily living, she felt fortunate to have a few minutes of uninterrupted pleasure.

She would awake clear-eyed and refreshed in the silence of the early morning and slip from her bed, making directly for Joe's nursery. The middle-of-the-night feedings, the stumbling from bed to crib, were a hazy memory, even though those events had taken place only a few hours earlier. It was in those hushed moments after rising that she really discovered the joy in motherhood.

For those privileged minutes she and the baby at her breast merged purely and completely. At such times she felt sure that she could do anything—*anything*—to safeguard his welfare. There was no force greater than that binding mother to child.

But Claire's special moments had been troubled in the past few weeks, disrupted in a way she did not understand. She would take her son from his crib, settle in the rocker, and put his supple mouth to her breast. But instead of the delicious questing of his velvety lips, she could feel his complete lack of interest in her nipple, his irate pulling away, as if he considered her nothing more than a nuisance.

His behavior puzzled her, and as he thrashed his head to avoid her nipple she felt the hot embers of anger in her veins—rage she had to fight. She wanted to shake him and demand that he tell her what was wrong.

It took a moment or two for her to quell her anger. She took deep breaths and told herself that she couldn't expose her anger to an innocent being, a guileless little baby who was unaware that he was upsetting the order of things in the adult world.

It did not take long for the good mother in Claire to take over. She held her son close and kissed him and whispered in his ear that she loved him above all things. The irritation passed, leaving behind a hurt bewilderment, a sense of not knowing what else she could do to please him.

But there was the fundamental, unavoidable fact: He would not take her milk. He laughed with her. He gurgled and cooed and squirmed and thrashed and loved her at her touch, but he was not interested in feeding and flourishing with his mother's milk.

She came down to breakfast puzzled and slightly disconcerted. Peyton was tidying up the kitchen. Emma had already left for school.

"Peyton," Claire asked, "have you noticed anything strange with Joe?"

Peyton shook her head. "No. He's been right on schedule with everything. Why? Is something wrong?"

"No . . . no . . ." said Claire. "Just wondering." She ran a hand through her hair. "Michael was up until four-thirty finishing his EPA proposal."

"I hope it works out," Peyton said absently. She was loading plates in the dishwasher.

Michael came bounding into the room. Despite his late night he looked eager and excited. He placed a manila envelope on the kitchen table. "Morning, everybody."

Peyton smiled at him. "Is there something I can get you? Something to eat?"

"Thanks," he said, "but no time. Got a meeting at the lab and I have to stop at Federal Express." He tapped the envelope. "Today is the day. This has to be in Washington tomorrow morning to make the EPA deadline."

"Why don't you let me send it for you, Michael?" Claire asked. "It's the last thing you need to worry about today. Peyton and I are going downtown, to the Botanical Gardens, so it wouldn't be a problem."

"Are you sure you'll have the time? It absolutely has to go out overnight." He seemed anxious not to let the precious packet of documents out of his sight.

"I'll take care of it."

Michael kissed his wife on the cheek. "Thanks, honey. Now I've got to get going."

Peyton had never been to the Seattle Botanical Gardens and was curious to see it. Claire talked about it constantly and in glowing terms. She had been volunteering there for years, and even though her family was growing, she still found time to do a few hours of work there every week.

Peyton found the humid and clammy air of the greenhouses rather oppressive, but Claire seemed to thrive on it, caring for the big plants with the same concern that she showed her children.

"It's sort of like a big botanist family down here," she explained. Peyton was sitting on a bench, watching Claire carefully, but occasionally glancing down at Joe, who lay in his portable crib. "All the people here sit around talking about fascinating topics like root rot and the drainage properties of shredded bark."

Peyton smiled and stroked Joe's hair. "It's good to have family," she said.

Claire carefully trimmed an aerial root from a large flowering plant.

"What's that?" Peyton asked.

"It's an orchid."

"I didn't know they got that big."

"This is a very rare species," said Claire. She sprayed it with a mister, her face a study in concentration. Joe was dozing off. At Peyton's feet was Claire's big shoulder bag, Michael's envelope just visible within it.

"This variety has to be kept damp at all times," Claire continued. "It's unable to store any moisture at all."

"I see," said Peyton.

Claire walked among the thicket of plants, lightly touching the clay pots and green branches. Where there was insufficient moisture, she doled out a little water with the mister.

"Will your greenhouse be similar to this one?" Peyton asked.

"I hope so, but on a much smaller scale." Claire was trimming one of the plants now, severing limbs with the precision of a surgeon. Quickly Peyton reached into Claire's purse and with the skill of a pickpocket lifted the envelope and slid it into her blouse. She glanced at Claire, who was still deep in her plants.

"I can't wait to see it." Peyton looked up into the upper reaches of the greenhouse. The top windows were open to the air; the wings of glass were cranked open by means of a complicated series of chains and pulleys.

Peyton was aware that the sound of clipping had stopped. She looked up to see Claire looking at her strangely, intensely. For a terrible moment she was afraid that Claire had seen her steal the envelope. She shifted uncomfortably.

"You know, Peyton," said Claire, "I can be a very good listener."

Peyton's guard was up immediately. "Yes . . . ?"

"I just wanted to let you know that if you ever want to talk about anything, I'm here."

"Talk about what?" Peyton looked at her wide-eyed, uncomprehending.

Now Claire felt uncomfortable, wishing she

hadn't brought up a delicate subject. "Well, it's just that you never speak about your husband. . . . I just thought . . ."

Peyton stared hard at her, as if she hadn't quite recognized the words that Claire had spoken to her. There was an awkward silence.

Claire was sure she had blundered. It was none of her business to cross the invisible line between employer and employee. She really had begun to feel as if Peyton were a member of the family. It was plain that Peyton did not share the sentiment.

"I'm sorry," Claire said with a shrug. "I shouldn't have brought it up."

Peyton was silent a long time. She thought about the absurdity of explaining the demise of her family to the very woman who had caused it. Then she started to speak, slowly, and with a faraway, slightly dazed expression on her face. It plainly hurt her to dredge up the memories.

"I was a just a kid when I met him," she said. "He was ten years older. He was very smart, very handsome, very charming." She turned the full intensity of her blue eyes on Claire. "And I worshiped him," she said matter-of-factly.

"Peyton . . ." Claire could see that she was in pain.

"He worshiped me," she continued. "He used

to say that the sun came out when I walked into the room. He took care of me. I was devastated when . . ."

"When?"

"When he was murdered."

Claire gasped, her gloved hand at her mouth. "Murdered? Oh, my God . . ."

Peyton's jaw had tightened and anger and anguish pulsed in her eyes. Her voice changed, a hard edge creeping into it. "They never caught who did it. But I firmly believe that what goes around comes around." She gazed at Claire. "Do you think that's true?"

"I hope so," said Claire.

"Me too." Peyton stood up and smiled. Her mood seemed to have changed completely. "There a bathroom around here?"

"Off the main lobby."

Peyton locked herself in the stall and took a deep breath and felt her cheeks flush. Anger throbbed through her veins. Talking about her husband's death with the very woman who had killed him had unleashed a fury in her that she did not trust herself to contain.

First, she took Michael's envelope from her blouse and angrily tore it into a dozen pieces. She tossed the bits into the toilet, pleased with her act of destruction. Claire, the perfect little wife, would be considerably less perfect by the time this day was done.

But she still felt the anger in her blood, and the destruction of the envelope had not slaked her thirst for revenge. Her hand curled into a fist and she smashed it into the steel walls of the stall, the thud echoing dully in the enclosed space. She kicked out, her foot denting the sides of the booth. Then she seized the brush next to the toilet and began pounding the metal walls, smashing the plastic handle into a dozen sharp shards.

Suddenly, as if she had been switched off, Peyton stopped. She was breathing hard, her shoulders rising and falling, her fury still thundering in her brain. She breathed deeply, bringing her pulse down, fighting to control her outrage.

It was a full five minutes before she trusted herself to leave the stall and rejoin Claire. Joe was awake and Claire had wrapped him up in a blanket and put him in his stroller. It was time to go.

Claire was still a little worried about Peyton. She hoped she hadn't pressed too hard on the old bruises of Peyton's tragic past. When Peyton emerged from the bathroom, she looked cool and poised, not a crack of strain showing.

"Are you okay?" Claire asked.

Peyton smiled radiantly. "Of course." She took her place behind the stroller.

A woman passing by peered in at Joe and smiled. "That's a beautiful baby you have there," she said.

"Thank you," Peyton said proudly.

Claire shot a glance at Peyton, wondering if she had heard correctly. Peyton's smile betrayed nothing.

Claire searched and re-searched her purse while the man at the Federal Express desk waited patiently.

"I need to send something overnight, but I can't seem to find it. I know it's here," said Claire. Her probing in her purse became a little more frantic. "I put it there this morning."

She felt panic rising in her and wheezed slightly, her lungs constricting. "I'm sorry," she stuttered. "I know it's—it can't be—"

But it was not there. Wheezing heavily now, she ran back to the car parked in front of the FedEx office.

"What's wrong?" asked Peyton, alarmed.

"I can't find Michael's envelope! Is it . . . do you see it on the floorboards? On the backseat?"

Peyton peered over the headrest. "It's not back there. I saw you put it in your purse."

"It's not there." Her breathing was harsh and labored as her asthma attack intensified.

"Claire, are you all right?"

Claire nodded and pulled open the glove compartment; seizing an inhaler, she shot the medication into her mouth. Slowly her breathing became more regular, but her face was pale with worry and concern.

"It's just my asthma," she said, still wheezing. "It'll pass. It just flares up when I get really upset."

Peyton stored this information in her brain. "It's going to turn up, Claire," she said soothingly. "We'll find it."

But they didn't. They retraced their route, searching the Botanical Gardens and tearing the house apart. The envelope was nowhere to be found.

By the time Michael got home from work, Claire was gray with worry and anxiety. She knew that her husband was not the kind of person who screamed and shouted and threw things when he got angry. In a sense, she wished he was—better to get it out in the open than be stoic. She couldn't bear the look of hurt and disappointment in his eyes, his furious silence and icy demeanor.

He shut her out all night, scarcely speaking

to her, as if the very sight of his wife annoyed him. Peyton kept a low profile that evening, withdrawing to her basement room as soon as dinner was done and cleared away. She lay on her bed and relished the irate hush from the upper floor.

At bedtime Claire made one last try at reconciliation.

"Michael," she said earnestly, "someone *must* have stolen it from my purse. It just disappeared. I've retraced all my steps, turned the house upside down. . . ."

Michael nodded wearily. All of her protests did not make up for the fact that a lot of work was down the drain. She had let him and his research team down.

Claire tried vainly to find some good news in the catastrophe.

"When you called the EPA, what did they say? Did they say they will accept it?"

Michael spoke in a monotone. "They said they would consider it in the next quarter. We'll have to wait three months before they even begin to appraise it."

"But will it be approved then?"

Michael sighed wearily. "We've been over this, Claire." He knew he had to do something, but he couldn't quite bring himself to embrace her. He patted her on the shoulder and then got into bed.

"Oh, Michael, I'm so sorry."

"I know you are, honey," he said listlessly. "It's going to be all right." He rolled over, turning his back to his wife.

"Michael—"

"Please, Claire. I'm very, very tired. . . ."

CHAPTER 12

Michael's hurt and irritation gradually wore off and had completely vanished by the time the Bartels and the Cravens and Peyton assembled in the auditorium of Emma's school for the annual class play.

In the tradition of tot shows, Emma and a dozen of her classmates had been cast as various types of vegetation, which, to their teacher's piano accompaniment, gradually grew from tiny seeds to strong trees. Great performance it was not, but to the beaming parents of all the little sprouts and woodland creatures, the actors deserved Academy Awards. Even the usually cynical Marlene got caught up in the excitement of the evening. She applauded as enthusiastically as the delighted parents, despite the fact she was dying for a cigarette.

When the show was over, the families and children and teachers mingled in the auditorium lobby. Marlene slipped away from the crowd into the open doorway, sneaking a smoke.

Emma was in the center of a group of admiring parents and teachers, but Peyton hung back, jogging Joe in her arms and whispering in his ear. She turned to see a woman bearing down on her. It was her friend from the park. Consternation crossed Peyton's face, and she looked around, searching for escape like a cornered animal.

"I didn't know you had a child here. Is she in Mrs. Henry's class? My daughter is in Mrs. Henry's class, too." Maybe the woman was new to the neighborhood and was looking to make a friend, but Peyton couldn't risk Claire and Michael catching her in a lie. "And here's your adorable little boy." The woman put out her hand to stroke Joe's head.

Peyton pulled him away quickly. "You must be mistaking me for someone else," she said coldly.

"But we spoke in the park last week. I'm *sure* it was you."

Peyton's eyes narrowed. "Are you calling me a liar?" she whispered nastily.

"No . . . no," the woman stammered, stunned by Peyton's odd behavior.

"Excuse me," Peyton said curtly. She walked to the group of people around Emma.

Claire took Joe from her arms. "How's he doing?"

"I think he's very tired," said Peyton. Her eyes strayed to the door. Marlene was watching her intently, as if trying to work out a complicated mystery to which Peyton was the only clue.

Emma was elated by the praise being heaped upon her. "Did you see me?" She clutched at the hem of Peyton's skirt. "Did you see me, Peyton?"

Peyton kissed Emma warmly. "I saw everything," she exclaimed. "You were terrific."

"She was great," said Marlene, walking over to them. "I mean, can we talk about raw talent for a moment? You blew those other sprouts right out of the water."

It took a while for Emma to go to sleep that night—the excitement from her performance and the praise had made her reluctant to go to bed. Eventually, however, sheer fatigue overcame her, and Claire came downstairs, delighted at her daughter's happiness.

Peyton was sitting in the living room when Claire entered. She settled on the couch, and the two women began talking comfortably in the twilight of the dark room. Their voices were hushed.

"Emma get to sleep?" Peyton asked.

"She finally passed out," said Claire with a smile.

"She certainly does love having Marlene and Marty around, doesn't she?" observed Peyton.

Claire nodded. "She has loved being around them since she was tiny. Marlene was the first person to make her smile."

"Marlene makes everyone smile. She's so . . ."

"So what?"

Peyton shrugged. "Glamorous, I guess."

Claire agreed. "She *is* glamorous, isn't she."

"Oh, very. She's definitely one of 'those' kind of women."

" 'Those' kind?" Claire asked quizzically. "What kind of woman is one of 'those' kind?"

"Oh, you know. She's always well put together, so chic, so elegant. Confident. You can just see the effect she has on men. Attracts men like a magnet."

"Yeah . . ." Claire considered this for a moment. Even at a children's play, Marlene had been perfectly groomed. Although she wore jeans and boots, she had been the most chic woman in the room, standing out amid the young mothers in their childproof clothing—smocks and caftans—many of them trying to hide bodies made stockier by childbearing.

"I hardly ever feel glamorous anymore," Claire said sadly, then stifled a yawn. "Well, I'm exhausted. I think I'll turn in."

"Good night," said Peyton.

The next morning Claire's disquiet had returned. Once again Joe refused her breast. Now she was really worried and decided it was time to share her fears with her husband. Michael was getting dressed when she entered the bedroom.

"Michael, I'm concerned about Joe."

Automatically he glanced at the intercom speaker on the dresser. Joe was gurgling and laughing to himself next door in his nursery. "What's wrong? He sounds happy enough."

"It's his eating habits."

"His eating habits?" Michael smiled. "What's the matter? Can't get enough?"

Claire was in no mood for kidding. The welfare of her child was at stake. "He doesn't want my breast the way he used to."

Michael's good humor vanished. "How long has this been going on?"

"About three weeks."

"Three weeks!"

"I'm afraid I'm going to lose my milk," said Claire plaintively.

"Let's call a doctor," said Michael.

"I did," Claire replied. "She said that as long as he continues to gain weight, we're okay."

"And is he? Gaining weight?"

Claire nodded. "But I don't see how. He's hardly eating anything at all."

Michael enfolded his wife in his arms. "Honey, I'm sure he's fine."

Claire allowed herself to be consoled, but deep in her soul she was uneasy, as if a shadow had fallen across her happy, sunny home.

Michael was as single-minded a scientist at work as he was a family man at home. By the time he got to the office and had donned his lab coat, thoughts of home, wife, and children were far from his mind. He was very surprised when his young assistant, Adam, touched him on the shoulder.

Michael was sitting at a computer screen, his fingers flying over the keyboard as he ran a series of DNA models through the electronic brain. He didn't even bother to look up.

"Read off the numbers, Adam," he said, "and I'll handle the input."

"It's not that, Michael. You have a visitor."

Michael looked up. Adam was sort of smirking at him, his eyebrows raised. "A visitor?" He never had visitors at work.

"Yeah, she's waiting in your office. Says her name is Peyton Flanders."

Now it was Michael's turn to raise his eyebrows. "Peyton! What's she doing here?"

"Didn't say. She is *really* good—"

"Yes. I know. She's our nanny, Adam."

Adam shrugged and grinned. "Uh-huh . . . okay. You should let me in on where you do your hiring."

"You have to have children before you hire a nanny," Michael tossed over his shoulder as he headed down the corridor.

When he entered his office, Peyton was reading the diplomas that decorated the walls. She gently rocked the stroller in which Joe lay sleeping. Michael immediately went to the baby carriage.

Peyton touched her lips with a finger. "He's out cold," she whispered. "I'm sorry to bother you here at work like this, but I wanted to speak to you in private."

Michael was concerned. "Is everything all right? Is there anything wrong at home?"

"No," Peyton whispered. "Everything's fine. It's just that I had an idea."

"An idea?"

She nodded. "It's something I've been thinking about for a couple of days."

"Let's hear it."

"Well, I happen to know that Claire's birthday is coming up and I thought it might be kind of nice to give her a surprise party. She's been kind of low lately. Especially since this whole thing with your proposal. You could invite all your friends. . . ."

Michael smiled. Peyton was a gem. She thought of everything. "That's a great idea. I think Claire would love it."

"Do you think Marlene would want to help out?"

"Help out? Are you kidding? She'll take over the whole thing."

"Maybe it's best not to tell her it was my idea," Peyton whispered.

"Why not?"

"I just don't want Marlene to think I'm being . . . competitive. You know, about Claire's friendship. I don't want her to get the wrong idea," she said innocently.

Michael smiled knowingly. "I guess you understand Marlene pretty well already."

Their whispers made this innocent conversation seem more intimate, even illicit. For a moment Peyton's gaze seemed to hold his. Then Michael pulled his eyes away, glancing over her shoulder into the lab. Adam was watching, a smirk still on his face.

The spell broke. "Well," said Peyton briskly, "I guess we should be on our way."

"Thanks for coming by." Michael leaned over the baby carriage and stroked his baby son's cheek. "Bye, little guy."

As he straightened, Peyton leaned in close to him, her arms lifting as if she were about to throw them around his neck and kiss him. Michael froze, like a small animal about to be attacked by a snake. Her hand brushed his shoulder.

She pulled a small white feather from his lab coat and looked at it closely, apparently oblivious to her boldness, her suggestiveness.

"Have you been plucking chickens?" she asked.

Michael laughed nervously and brushed at his shoulders. "No, not today anyway. I wonder where that came from."

Peyton let the feather fall. She pushed the stroller to the office door and Michael opened it for her.

"See you at home," said the nanny.

Michael Bartel (MATT McCOY) and his beautiful wife, Claire (ANNABELLA SCIORRA)

Michael Bartel and his young daughter Emma (MADELINE ZIMA) pass a happy morning together, singing.

Claire's first meeting with the beautiful Peyton Flanders (REBECCA DE MORNAY)

Hired handyman Solomon (ERNIE HUDSON) is the only one who suspects that Peyton might not be what she seems.

LEFT: Peyton Flanders quickly becomes a part of the Bartel household.

BELOW: Claire accepts Peyton as a devoted and responsible mother's helper, without question.

RIGHT: Peyton easily wins the affection of young Emma.

BELOW: In no time, Peyton's friendly demeanor enables her to become a fixture in Claire's home.

Michael, Emma and Peyton spend time together—without Claire.

Peyton's helpful pose conceals a much darker plan.

ABOVE: Peyton reveals the violent side of her nature.

RIGHT: Young Emma turns to Peyton for comfort when her mother causes a scene.

ABOVE: The Bartels' close friend, Marlene (JULIANNE MOORE) finds evidence that Peyton is not who she seems to be.

RIGHT: Claire's beautiful greenhouse will become a part of Peyton's terrifying plan.

LEFT: Solomon attempts to rescue Claire's newborn son, Joe.

BELOW: Claire finds her children and Solomon in the attic.

"Bye."

Every head in the lab turned and watched as Peyton pushed the carriage along the corridor and out the door.

CHAPTER 13

Solomon loved to work. It pleased him to show the world that he was competent. When he had arrived at the Bartels' house, he knew he would encounter resistance; he knew that "normal" people would always think him incapable of succeeding at anything. He spent every hour of every day proving himself. Through his work he erased the misgivings of the doubters and demonstrated his expertise.

Solomon particularly liked working for the Bartels. They had welcomed him into their home, made him feel wanted, given him the family he had never had. He would like to have been able to hold Joe in his arms, just once, and his inability to do so bothered him and hurt him a little, but it was a small price to pay. One day Joe would be Emma's size and he could play with him the way he played with the little girl—romping on the lawn and laughing together over private, silly jokes. Solomon could wait for the future.

He took his work on the trim of the Bartels' house very seriously, laying down layer after layer of paint on the intricate Victorian fretwork. The contrast between the pale cream of the house and these deep green accents was pleasing to the eye and he was very proud.

He had done all of the lower trim and was now working on the upper stories. Today, he decided, was the day to work on the delicate latticework high up near the peaked roof.

Solomon steadied a tall wooden ladder against the side of the house and climbed up. One hand grasped the rungs; the other held a can of paint and a narrow brush. He climbed carefully and slowly until he was level with the window of the nursery.

He looked away from the window, faintly guilty, as if afraid of being accused of being a Peeping Tom. But he *did* want to catch a glimpse of baby Joe, who was probably sleeping in his crib.

Slightly ashamed of himself, he peered in the window. He could make out the crib, and through its rails he could see that it was empty. Solomon frowned. That was odd. He knew Claire wasn't home and that this was the baby's usual nap time. . . .

Then he saw the rocker. Sitting in the chair was Peyton, her blouse undone, with Joe locked happily, hungrily at her breast. Her eyes were closed and her head was thrown back in abandon, her beautiful face soft with bliss.

Solomon stared and felt fear gushing through his veins. His knowledge of babies and motherhood was muddled and fragmentary, but he *was* sure that only the mother should give milk to the baby. Anything else was unnatural.

Peyton scared him; she always had. From the very first time they had met, when he had stained her blouse with the paint, he knew that she hated him, that she considered him her enemy. Deep in his soul he felt she was evil. He also knew she would destroy him in an instant if she got the chance.

Solomon hesitated for a moment and then decided he had to get away from there. Quickly he started down the ladder, but before he cleared the window frame, the paint can clanked loudly against the shingle of the house. He froze and looked into the room. Peyton's eyes opened and locked on his. They stared at each other for a moment. Then she looked away, gathering her blouse over her exposed breasts.

Solomon hurried down the ladder. On the ground he looked back at the window, as if he expected to see her there. Instead all he saw were the closed nursery windows. Upset and perplexed, Solomon tried to busy himself with other tasks, but he could not erase from his mind the unsettling image of Peyton with Joe at her breast.

Anxiety took hold of him. He didn't know what to do; he could not think straight. He wasn't sure he could tell Michael and Claire about what he had seen—he would be nervous and tongue-tied and he would get the story wrong. Peyton would call him a liar. . . . They might send him away.

"Solomon!"

He jumped and turned. Emma was standing behind him, smiling happily. It was as if the sun had come out on a cloudy day.

"Is it three o'clock already?" Solomon tried to make his voice sound light and bright.

"I want to show you my sculpture!" Emma was holding a bright red papier-mâché blob.

Solomon took the paper lump from the little girl and turned it over and over in his hands, examining it closely. "It's so nice."

"See," said Emma happily, "it's part lion and part bird."

"Uh-huh."

"This is the front."

"I see," said Solomon seriously. "Is this a tail or is it a foot?" He pointed to a bulge in the side of the blob.

"That's part of the fur!" said Emma indignantly.

"Of course," said Solomon slowly. "I see now. This is a piece of art, Emma."

Emma beamed. "I *knew* you'd understand."

"Hello, Emma. Hello, Solomon." Peyton had come out of the house as if to welcome the little girl home.

"Hi, Peyton. Look at my sculpture."

Peyton scarcely glanced at it. She kept her eyes on Solomon. He felt himself tense up, blood rushing to his face. He licked his lips nervously.

"Emma, go on inside. I want to have a word with Solomon."

"Okay." Obediently Emma ran off.

Peyton moved in close to Solomon, cornering him against the house. He shrunk away from her, as if she were the devil.

"Are you a retard?" she asked. Her voice was low with menace. She smiled, but there was naked intimidation in her eyes.

Solomon seemed to quiver nervously, avoiding her gaze and trying to ignore her question. "Please leave me alone," he managed to stammer.

"I asked, are you a retard?"

"N-n-no . . ."

She leaned in even closer. He recoiled, almost pulling his neck into his body like a turtle. He could smell her perfume and her breath was sweet on his face.

"Are you toilet-trained, *retard*?"

All of a sudden Solomon's fear vanished. In its place came a white-hot rage. He hated her. He hated that she was insulting him, robbing him of his dignity. He hated what she was doing to his family, his friends. He was so angry he could not speak. His big hands curled into huge, hard fists.

She looked at his fists and mocked him with her eyes. "Go ahead," she said. "Hit me. That would suit my plans very nicely."

Solomon could see exactly what she was thinking. His hands loosened. He could not allow himself to lose control. That would only lead to disaster.

"Don't mess with me," she whispered. "Retard."

"I—I won't let you hurt them," he stammered. "They are my friends."

"Like I say, don't mess with me. And don't get any ideas about telling them what you saw. No one will believe you, do you understand? Tell them what you saw and I'll tell them what *I* saw. My story will be . . . better. Understand?"

Solomon stood stock-still.

"I said, *understand*?"

Solomon managed to nod.

"Good," said Peyton. She stalked away from him without a backward glance.

It was the end of the day and Solomon was packing his enormous tool case. His bike and cart were standing in front of the garage and he was stowing his hammers and screwdrivers, clean brushes and wrenches in his wagon. This was something he had been doing for as long as he could remember. He lay the tools in the box with extreme precision, a longtime ritual that somehow reassured him. Today, however, it did not have its usual comforting effect.

His heart was heavy and he was tormented with anxiety. He couldn't tell the Bartels what he had seen—Peyton would quickly turn the story against him—but at the same time he felt like a traitor, who knew something was harming his best friends in the world, but was powerless to help them.

Michael appeared in the side door of the

garage, his hands in his pockets and looking deeply troubled. A jolt of fear shot through Solomon. Peyton had done something—he could feel it in his bones.

"Hey, Solomon, got a moment?"

Solomon winced. "Y-yes . . ."

"Come into the garage."

"Okay." Solomon walked the few yards to the garage, like a condemned man going to the gallows, trying desperately to ready himself for the horrible scene he was sure would unfold.

Nothing prepared him for what happened next. Claire and Emma were waiting with Michael. As soon as he entered the garage, they shouted and stepped inside. For a moment Solomon couldn't quite focus on the thing they had revealed. Something gleaming and crimson registered in his brain. Then he saw it clearly. In the middle of the garage stood a bright red bicycle, a shiny basket looped over the handlebars and a big red bow tied to the seat.

"Surprise!"

Solomon's brown eyes swam with tears. Michael wheeled the bike toward him and put his hands on the white plastic grips.

"This is for you, big guy."

Emma capered around the room, clapping her hands and laughing happily.

Solomon was overwhelmed with emotion.

"You . . . you are my friends," he said, hoarse with tears.

"Of course we are," said Claire. "We're all friends here."

Peyton, whom no one had thought to ask to the celebration, stood very still on the porch, listening to the happy voices floating across the backyard. She knew that Solomon would not tell the Bartels that he had seen her nursing Joe; she had intimidated him far too thoroughly for that. But now that she saw how much they really loved him, how Emma doted on the childlike man, she made up her mind.

She would have to destroy him.

CHAPTER 14

"You should have seen his face when we gave him the bike," said Claire.

She and Peyton were in the basement laundry room, next to Peyton's room. They were folding and smoothing the clean clothes, reducing a tall jumble of tangled clothing to two neat piles.

"I can imagine." Peyton glanced out the window. "That's quite an . . . an involved game they're playing."

The window over the washing machine was at eye level with the rear lawn of the house. Solomon and Emma were wrestling and tumbling together in the sweet grass. The air was filled with Emma's happy giggles. She screamed and chortled when Solomon started to tickle her, swatting at his questing fingers, laughing so hard she could hardly draw breath. Claire looked at her daughter, felt her happiness, and beamed.

The almost-finished frame of the greenhouse, lacking only glass, stood in the rear of the yard.

"Emma just adores him," said Claire.

Peyton paused for a moment, as if hesitant. Claire sensed her indecision and looked at her quizzically. "Is there something on your mind, Peyton?"

Peyton drew a deep breath. "Claire, this may be none of my business, but I've been observing some behavior that . . . behavior that might be inappropriate."

Claire shook her head and blanched. "What do you mean, 'inappropriate'?"

Peyton ran her hand through her hair, as if unsure of whether or not to continue. "I guess it's sort of touchy-feely stuff. I'm sure I'm wrong. I *know* how much you trust Solomon."

Claire's features were set and hard, her voice cold. "You must have misunderstood. Solomon would never do such a thing."

Peyton nodded and smiled reassuringly. "You're right. I'm sure you're right. It would be obvious if Emma were keeping a secret like that. I apologize for bringing it up."

"I'm glad you did," said Claire. She was

chewing on her lower lip, thinking hard. Then she started out of the room. "Would you mind finishing up? I forgot something. . . ."

Peyton turned back to her laundry, smiling to herself. She picked up a pair of Emma's tiny panties, pale blue with a small pink bow at the waistband. She folded them and then slipped them into the pocket of her blue jeans. The seed of doubt had been planted; now it was time to make it grow.

Like a loose tooth or a faint but perceptible ache, Claire was aware of Peyton's words all that afternoon and into the evening. The horrible possibility of Solomon molesting her daughter seemed to hover like a storm cloud in her mind. She convinced herself—twice—that Solomon's attentions were out of line; she was *sure* that his actions were not innocent. . . . Then she would remember Emma's exhilarated laughter, the way her eyes lit up when he appeared, and she would convince herself that there was nothing between them except love and innocent play.

She tried to remember everything she had ever heard about child molesting. She shuddered at the recollection that infants were often irreparably damaged, that it cast a shadow over their whole lives. They were scarred and scared,

ashamed over something they could not control. But she also remembered reading somewhere that such children were withdrawn, tac-
iturn, and unsociable, that they would never,
by choice, associate with their abuser. That was
certainly not her little girl. She sought Solomon
out, always trying to divert him from his work
to play with her. No, she decided finally, Peyton
had been mistaken. Perhaps the trauma of her
own past made her unnaturally vigilant, sens-
ing threats where there were none.

And yet . . .

That night, when Claire went to tuck her little
girl into bed, she could not stop herself from
probing a little in the hope of discovering something. After all, Peyton would not have brought
up such a serious subject without some grounds
for suspicion.

Emma was settled in her bed, her little doll
tucked into the crook of her arm, her eyelids
heavy with sleep. Claire sat on the edge of her
bed and smoothed her daughter's brow.

"I love you very much; you know that, don't
you, sweetheart?" Claire's voice was gentle,
soothing.

Emma nodded. "Uh-huh."

"And you know that if something happened,
good or bad, you could tell me and it wouldn't

matter. You know I would love you anyway. No matter what."

"Uh-huh."

Emma's eyes were wide and serious now and she was listening intently to her mother. For a moment Claire worried that she was scaring her little girl.

But she pressed on. "Because we shouldn't have any secrets, Emma. Secrets between people who love each other are bad." She took Emma's little face between her hands. "Do you understand?"

Emma's brow was furrowed in worry. Of course, she had secrets with Peyton—they had a whole secret club. She ached to tell her mother, but she couldn't bring herself to break her vow.

Claire saw clearly that her daughter was very troubled by something. "What is it, baby?"

"Nothing," Emma said in a subdued voice.

Claire stroked her brow, soothing her distressed daughter.

"You know what day tomorrow is?"

"Uh-huh. It's greenhouse day."

"That's right. And you will be there to help me, right?"

"Will I still be in charge of the strawberries?" Something in Emma's voice suggested that she was afraid she might be punished for something, that somehow she had gotten in trouble with her mother.

"Of course, darling."

Reassured, Emma snuggled down in the bed. Claire, lost in thought, stayed with her until she fell asleep.

It had only taken a day or two for Solomon and a couple of workmen hired from a construction company to lay the foundation for the greenhouse and to erect the wooden frames from the Botanical Gardens. The more complicated work of installing the hardware that controlled the opening and closing of the roof panes had to be done by glaziers hired for the day.

The workers arrived promptly the next morning and set about placing the glass in the framework. The walls of the greenhouse were made of fiberglass sheets, which admitted light but which couldn't actually be seen through. Only the roof would have clear glass, set in wings that would be opened or closed with a pulley-and-chain system.

Emma was puzzled by the translucent sheets. "How come I can't see through this glass?"

"That's fiberglass, honey." Claire was kneading the moist dirt in a tub with a small tool.

She put it aside and stood up, dusting off the knees of her blue jeans.

"I thought greenhouses were *all* glass."

"Not always," Claire explained patiently. "If this one was all glass, it would get too hot in here and the sun would scorch the plants." She grasped the wheel by the door that controlled the wings and tried to turn it. It was old and worn and difficult to turn. "The ceiling will be clear glass because that lets in the sun better. But you have to be careful not to touch the clear glass, because that's too sharp."

Emma appraised the brickwork floor of the greenhouse. She picked up Claire's sharp-edged miniature shovel and toyed with it. "Where are the strawberries going to go?"

Claire was still wrestling with the recalcitrant gear wheel. "The strawberries are going to be next to the herb garden." She glanced at her daughter. "Emma, put the shovel down. It's not a plaything."

"Okay." Emma put the shovel aside and went outside. "Hi, Solomon!"

Solomon was high up on his ladder, painting the trim at the uppermost peak of the roof. He waved and smiled.

Peyton came out of the house, Joe on her hip, his intercom in her other hand. She watched a moment while Claire continued to struggle with the wheel. There was a brake gear on the whole mechanism, a safety feature that prevented the chain from shooting through the housing and closing the windows suddenly. Old and almost rusted shut, it was the reason the whole thing wasn't working properly. Claire hit it with the heel of her hand and the cog gave, the wheel lurching. The windows attached to the suddenly released chain slammed closed. Luckily no glass was in the frame.

"Claire," Peyton asked, "Joe's intercom konked out and I couldn't find any batteries in the house. Do you think Solomon's got any in his camper?"

Claire was still frowning at the machinery. "Probably. He's got everything else in there." The wagon that Solomon trailed behind his bike was something of a family joke. He was obsessively determined to have every tool for every job, and Michael and Claire—with Solomon's permission—had taken to looking in there when they needed anything, from an extension cord to a sledgehammer.

Peyton nodded and started toward the garage, stopping to hike Joe into a more comfortable position. Claire took off her gloves and tossed them aside.

"You've got your hands full," she said. "Let me take a look for you."

She strolled into the garage, pausing a moment to allow her eyes to adjust to the gloom. She opened the lift top of the wagon and pushed aside the first drawer of tools. She stared into the second drawer, her eyes widening in horror. Nestled among the oily, gleaming tools was a pair of Emma's panties, the pale blue ones with the pink bow on the waistband.

Claire felt as if she had been punched in the chest. She grabbed the panties from the drawer, staggered back a few feet, and then turned.

Someone was standing in the doorway. Claire screamed. Solomon, at the entrance, dropped his paint can and screamed, too. Green paint spilled across the concrete floor. Claire pushed by him and ran.

Peyton was dashing across the lawn and caught Claire in her arms. "What happened? What's going on?"

Claire was wheezing. She could feel her chest tightening and the panic rising within her. She clutched the panties in her hands. She felt sick to her stomach.

"It's Solomon," she panted. "He's been molesting Emma." A shiver of revulsion rocked her. "Oh, my God . . ."

"Claire! Calm down!"

"All those horrible games . . ."

Peyton held her close, playing mother to her

daughter. Claire was almost doubled over in her arms, fighting for breath, the wheezing harsh and high in her throat.

"It's okay. . . . It's okay," said Peyton. "Come into the house and get an inhaler." She guided Claire up the porch steps.

At the backdoor she looked over her shoulder. Solomon was standing in front of the garage watching them. He was trembling. Peyton looked at him for a moment, a smile of triumph on her lips.

Michael left work immediately and was at home by the time the two representatives from the Better Day Society showed up at the house. They stood in the front yard talking quietly, Solomon standing with them, his head bowed contritely, a picture of misery.

"Now, suppose you tell us what happened, Solomon." The director of the Better Day Society was an older man with iron-gray hair and a kind voice.

"Mr. Hopkins . . ." Solomon's mouth worked and twisted as he desperately tried to speak. "I—I—I, sh-sh-she . . . I'm . . . I can't . . ."

"Did you hurt the little girl?" asked the other man from the Better Day Society.

"Nooo! I l-love her!"

Michael looked away.

"Did you touch her?"

Sadly Solomon nodded. "When—when—when we played the games."

"The games?"

"The w-w-wrestling game."

The three men exchanged glances. Hopkins and his associate looked at the ground.

"Mr. Bartel, I'm very sorry about this. We had no idea that Solomon would ever do anything like this. It's a tragedy. I am truly sorry."

Michael was a mass of conflicting emotions. One part of him wanted to take Solomon in his hands and break every bone in his body. Another part of him pitied the man. He was a child in a man's body, hardly aware of the difference between right and wrong. One thing, however, was clear to him.

"Solomon," he said firmly. "You have to leave here."

Solomon's eyes widened in alarm and suddenly he had control of his words. "*Please*. What did I do wrong?"

"Okay, Solomon," said Mr. Hopkins. "We have to go now." He took Solomon by the wrist and started leading him toward the gate he had built. Solomon allowed himself to be pushed a few feet, then he dug in his heels.

"Claire!" he shouted. "Please don't let them

take me! Where's Emma? Emma! Emma, help me!"

Emma flew to the window of the living room, tears streaming from her eyes. "Solomon! Why are they taking you away?" Claire tried to get her away from the window.

"Mommy," Emma cried. "I don't understand. Why are those men taking Solomon away?"

Claire felt she was fast approaching her breaking point. "Honey," she pleaded, "please come away from the window. Emma, please!"

Emma turned from the window, tears coursing down her face. She shoved her mother aside and ran from the room, sobbing as she went.

"Emma!"

The little girl ran through the kitchen and out the backdoor. Claire felt the sharp stabs of jealousy and betrayal as her daughter bolted across the lawn and into the arms of Peyton, who was sitting in the afternoon sun, Joe lying on a blanket at her side.

The front door slammed and a moment later Michael came into the room. He stood behind her. "Well," he said, "that's done."

Claire turned to him, hoping for solace, but saw that his face was cold and stony. The tension in the air was palpable.

"My God," she whispered. "You think this is my fault."

"I didn't say that."

"I brought him into the house and I let it happen, right? That's what you're thinking, isn't it?"

"Of course it's not your fault, Claire," Michael snapped. "I'm just upset. Am I allowed to be upset?"

Claire felt her lips trembling and was on the verge of dissolving into tears. "How could I have known?" she pleaded. "You didn't pick up on anything either."

"I'm not here all day," he said shortly. "I can't do everything myself."

Anger elbowed aside her anguish. "What the hell is that supposed to mean?"

"It means I'm not here. I can't be. I have *work* to do."

"And I don't?" she replied quickly. "I have the greenhouse. I have the Botanical Gardens—"

"Volunteer work." There was almost a sneer in his voice.

"It's still *work*," she said angrily. "And I have the children."

"And you have Peyton," he said.

Their voices carried outside, and Emma, seeking refuge from their angry words, burrowed deeper into Peyton's embrace. "Why do Mommy and Daddy have to fight?"

Peyton stroked her hair. "It's just that everybody's upset about Solomon, that's all."

Emma turned her face to Peyton's. "But I don't understand. What did Solomon do?"

Peyton shrugged. "I guess your mommy didn't like Solomon very much. So they came and took him away." She never missed a chance to set Emma against her mother.

"But that's not fair!"

"Sometimes things aren't fair at all," Peyton said softly.

"I like Solomon," said Emma despondently.

"I know you do. I wanted to help Solomon, but I was afraid your mommy would send me away, too. . . ."

Emma felt a flash of fear and hugged Peyton closer. "She can't do that!" Her voice was alive with alarm. "I won't let her send you away!"

"Don't worry, Emma. I'm staying right here with you. No matter what."

Emma was silent for a long time, trying to sort out the disturbing events of that long sorrowful day. She thought about all that happened. Solomon was gone and she couldn't see why. Her father was unhappy and she didn't know why. The only common denominator in the whole thing was her mother. She was the villain.

"I hate her," she said finally. "I bet your mommy wasn't mean like mine is."

"I didn't have a mommy. She died when I was very little," Peyton said gently.

The very thought horrified Emma. Her eyes grew wide and she gasped. "Your mommy *died*? But then who took care of you?"

Peyton was matter-of-fact. "I had to take care of myself."

"Peyton," Emma asked very seriously. "If something happened to my mommy, would you take care of me?"

"Of course I would." Peyton glanced up at the house and listened to the angry voices for a moment. "And your daddy, too."

CHAPTER 15

The next weeks were difficult and perplexing for the whole family, but no one took it harder than Claire. Michael could bury himself in his work, but every day Claire was confronted with the reminders of the tragedy that had befallen her home. Her nerves were frayed, and the smallest annoyance was more than she could handle.

She carried an immense burden of guilt. Michael had told her over and over again that he did not hold her responsible for Emma's problem. But she bore the shame like a secret wound and she compensated for it by trying to be perfect, the consummate wife with a flawless home. An attitude like that did nothing for her mental health—and it didn't take much to set her off.

One morning, when she and Peyton were making the bed in the master bedroom, Claire found that she could not quite get the perfect hospital corner on her side. She tried and tried, but the linen would just not tuck properly. She felt her anger rising and became even more clumsy. Peyton's hands flew smoothly over the sheets.

"Dammit!" Claire said angrily, slapping down the sheets.

Peyton looked at her, pity in her eyes. She patted the bed.

"Sit down."

Claire sighed and sat, Peyton settling next to her, their thighs touching. Peyton took Claire's hand in hers. "Emma is going to be fine," she said quietly. "Trust me."

Claire tried to calm herself down. "The child therapist says it's normal that she wouldn't be able to say what happened at first. Children have trouble verbalizing these things." She repeated the pat conclusion of the therapist as if it were a reassuring prayer.

"Of course they do," said Peyton.

But Claire couldn't stop herself from brooding over Emma's ordeal. She tried to shut out the details of what happened between her daughter and Solomon, but grotesque images flashed in her mind like slides.

"I just hate her having to go over it again and again. It tears me up inside." Tears were in her eyes now.

"Claire . . ." Peyton stroked her back as if she were trying to massage sympathy into her.

"And she's so different around me lately," said Claire, plainly agitated. "She's been acting guarded and angry. She's always cautious and wary. Like she's afraid of me. It's as if—do you think she blames me because I didn't protect her?" A tear dribbled down her cheek.

"Shhh . . ." Peyton murmured. She stroked Claire's back a little harder. "Try to relax."

Claire gave in and sank slowly backward onto the bed, turning onto her stomach. Her back was rigid with the strain of the last few days. Peyton's fingers dug into the muscle and flesh, breaking up the pockets of anxiety, seeming to relax the tension.

Peyton pushed herself up on her knees, kneeling over Claire's back and bearing down on her, stroking deep and regularly, warmly, soothingly.

A delicious wave of release seemed to break over Claire. She nestled into the bed and closed her eyes. "Mmm, that feels good. So good . . ."

Peyton's knowing fingers caressed their way

down Claire's spine, working at the kinks. Claire wriggled languorously under her touch, feeling herself melt. She suddenly realized how little she had been touched in recent weeks. There seemed to be a barrier between her and her husband. His embraces had been perfunctory, not cold, exactly, but distant.

Her breathing now deep and calm, she smiled to herself. The smooth, warm comfort of touch did more than loosen her muscles; she found herself becoming loquacious as Peyton's fingers gracefully stroked her neck.

"There's something you don't know about," she murmured. "Something you don't know about . . . Another reason why this happening to Emma is so devastating."

Peyton's hands had slipped into Claire's soft hair, gently massaging her scalp.

"Now, what is that?" she asked, her voice low, as if speaking too loud would ruin the mood.

"I was molested. Nine months ago. By a doctor . . . Like Solomon, someone I thought I could trust."

The massage stopped for just a moment, but Claire didn't notice. Peyton felt her stomach churning and her cheeks flushing. In all the time she had been with the Bartels, neither

Claire nor Michael had ever mentioned their experience with her late husband.

"How awful," said Peyton. Her hands crept under Claire's shirt and touched the warm skin. She pushed the material beyond her bra strap, undid the narrow band, and slipped off the shoulder straps. Her hands snaked up to Claire's delicate neck and circled it. Peyton's lip curled and her eyes became hard. Right then she could have broken Claire's neck. Her anger was welling within her. But she would wait until it was time. . . .

"I feel like Michael thinks it's partially my fault. He's never said anything, but I have the feeling—"

"Your fault? Why on earth would he think a thing like that?"

"I didn't scream. I didn't do anything. I just took it. I froze."

Peyton's long nails traveled down from Claire's shoulders to the base of her back and then around her waist. Claire raised her hips slightly as if giving a green light to more intimacy.

"Sometimes . . ." Claire said dreamily. "Sometimes I think he wonders if I let it happen."

Peyton leaned forward, her breasts grazing Claire's back, her lips breathy in Claire's ear.

"Did you?" she whispered. "Did you let it happen?"

Claire shook her head. "I was afraid of him. He was a . . . he was a monster."

Their faces were so close together they seemed almost on the verge of kissing. "It must have been terrible for you," Peyton said huskily.

"Yes. The whole thing was an ordeal. Disgusting. He was loathsome."

Peyton had heard enough. She glided off Claire's back, as if slipping from a saddle. She walked out of the room, leaving Claire lying facedown, her shirt pulled up to her breasts. Claire propped herself up on her elbows and looked over her shoulder at Peyton. Claire's hair was messy, her breathing heavy, her face flushed.

Like a hunter stalking prey, Peyton began closing in. The jaws of the trap were beginning to close, the meticulously constructed snare was about to clamp around her enemy and destroy her. Peyton had struck a blow to the household by banishing Solomon, had poisoned the trust between mother and child. Now it was time to ruin the relationship between Michael and Claire. She knew exactly which weapon in her arsenal she would use—jealousy.

Michael managed to have a few quick, quiet words with Peyton about the surprise party.

"Marlene wants to get together sometime today or tonight to make up a guest list. But I'm not sure anymore that we should go ahead with the party. What do you think?"

Peyton had to pretend to consider this question, but she knew exactly what her answer would be. "I think we should go ahead," she said after apparently thinking for a moment. "Everyone could use some cheering up around here. In fact, I'd say Claire needs it more now than ever. You know how she's been blaming herself."

Michael nodded. "I think you're right, Peyton. I guess I just needed to hear it. I'll go call Marlene."

"Do that," said Peyton.

She went downstairs quickly, snatching up a pile of folded laundry, and hurried up to the second story, meeting Claire as she came out of the nursery.

"I've got some things for Michael, but I didn't want to disturb him. He's in the bedroom and he's got the door closed."

"That's okay." Claire took the laundry. "I'll take it in."

Marlene was a busy woman and it took a few minutes for Michael and her to figure out a meeting time that was convenient for both of them. Michael suggested lunch, but Marlene demurred—she was having lunch with Claire that day. They settled on seven-thirty that night. If Claire had heard any of the beginning of the conversation, she would have recognized it as perfectly innocent. Instead, as she opened the bedroom door, she caught only a single incriminating fragment.

"No, no, she doesn't suspect a thing," Michael said, laughing. He was hunched over the phone, his back to the door. "But it's probably not a good idea to talk here. I'll call you later from the lab."

With elaborate care, Claire placed the laundry on the bed, then straightened the bedspread, patting out the faintest of wrinkles. Blood throbbed in her temples and she could feel anxiety welling up in her.

Michael had put the phone down quickly, guiltily, and was pretending to be deeply engrossed in the selection of a jacket. He removed a blue blazer, a slightly more formal choice than he would normally have worn to the laboratory.

"Who were you talking to?" Claire asked—nonchalantly, she hoped.

"Huh?"

"On the phone. Just now."

"I, uh, I was talking to . . . Adam. At the lab."

"Oh." Claire was still patting the same spot on the bed.

"As a matter of fact, you should know that I'll have to work pretty late tonight. There's some . . . there's some trouble with the tetracycline tests."

"I see," said Claire. Her voice was a monotone. "You'll be late."

"Yes." Michael slipped on his stylish blazer and kissed his wife on the cheek. "Don't wait up."

He headed quickly for the door, as if he was eager to escape his wife's presence.

Claire remained where she was, straightening and restraightening the bed, her gaze fixed, her thoughts in chaos.

CHAPTER 16

Several times during lunch with Marlene that day, Claire found herself on the verge of revealing her suspicions about Michael's infidelity. Several things held her back, a mixture of practical reasons and superstitions. She couldn't bring herself to say out loud, "I think Michael is having an affair." She could taste the statement on her lips, but she couldn't say it. It was as if she were restrained by some supernatural force, as if saying it would make it real. Claire could not confess her fears to her closest friend because she was embarrassed to admit that she could not hold her man, as if his infidelity were somehow her fault.

Claire could not tell because she would not

have been able to stand the pitying look in Marlene's eye. The pity would have been followed by righteous anger and then by Marlene's natural tendency to take charge. She would have outlined strategies for winning him back. Or she would have inundated Claire with advice on divorce—naming lawyers, outlining separation agreements and divorce settlements. By the time coffee was served, she would have worked out child visitation rights and alimony, and put their house up for sale at the fair market price.

Marlene would have been a friend, helping as she thought she should, but unspoken would have been her disquiet—is infidelity contagious; was her own marriage threatened?—or her relief, as if some plague had passed by her house and struck some other.

So Claire sat through lunch with an imperturbable look on her face, dutifully ordering a salad and refusing a glass of wine, pretending to be shocked when Marlene ordered herself a second.

She smiled when she thought a smile was called for, laughing from time to time as her companion tossed off one of her trademark barbed witticisms. But she did not taste her food, attended only minimally to Marlene's talk, her mind all the while in a whirl.

She went through the rest of the afternoon mechanically. The two women went shopping at the Factoria Mall, trawling for clothes at Nordstrom's and Neiman-Marcus. She scarcely noticed when Marlene spent hundreds of dollars on a pair of boots at I. Magnin and bought half a dozen hardcover books at Doubleday. She put up with Marlene's good-natured teasing when Claire insisted on stopping at a nursery to buy three bags of loamy-smelling mulch. But she went through her day like an automaton, her mind never once straying from the painful territory of her suspicions.

Claire was relieved when she finally pulled her Volvo wagon into the driveway of her own house.

"You sure you don't want me to drop you off?"

"Nope," said Marlene, getting out of the car. "I can walk two blocks, even in heels." She gave Claire a little peck on the cheek. "Thanks for everything. I especially liked the part where we picked up the fertilizer."

"Mulch," corrected Claire.

"Whatever."

Peyton came out of the house, Joe in her arms. "Hello, you two."

Marlene pointedly ignored the greeting, directing her attentions to Joe. "This little man

ROBERT TINE

gets more handsome every time I see him."
While Claire started to unload the car Marlene
took the baby from Peyton and kissed and cooed
over him. But Joe was tired and cranky.

"Claire," said Peyton, "let me give you a
hand." As she leaned into the car and seized
one of the twenty-five-pound bags, something
caught her eye. Marlene's purse was lying on
the backseat, her expensive gold cigarette
lighter gleaming. Quickly Peyton grabbed it
and stuffed it in her pocket.

"He's growing so fast. It's like he's a different
kid every time I see him. Hey, what's the matter, little guy?" Joe's face was wrinkling into a
fit of bad-tempered crying. Marlene's maternal
skills were taxed to the limit. She looked to
Claire for deliverance from the unhappy bundle
in her arms.

"Here . . . Give him to me." Claire took her
son in her arms and jogged him gently. This
seemed to infuriate him even more and he redoubled his wailing.

Marlene pretended to cover her ears. "He sure
has got a great set of lungs, hasn't he?"

Claire tried to hush her baby, whispering in
his ear and bobbing him in one arm. "It's okay,
honey, it's okay."

But Joe refused to be comforted. He wriggled
and struggled in his mother's arms, his face red

and wet with tears. Peyton edged into the picture, having deposited her heavy bag of mulch next to the car.

"I don't know what's gotten into him today." She held out her arms. "Let me try."

Joe climbed into her arms and nestled against her. Peyton held him close and, whispering in his ear, gently shushed him. His crying lessened immediately and he smiled. Marlene looked to Claire, then to Peyton, then back to Claire. It was an awkward, silent moment, broken only by the gentle tinkle of the wind chimes hanging outside the nursery window.

"What," asked Marlene archly, "is that annoying noise?"

"Wind chimes." Claire pointed to the window. "They were a gift from Peyton."

Marlene smiled. "Oops. Well, I'm sure they're charming. I'm off." She started toward the street.

Suddenly Claire didn't want to be alone. "Marlene," she said impulsively. "Peyton is making one of her famous desserts tonight. Why don't you bring Marty over later for a taste. Michael's going to be late tonight, so I thought . . ."

Marlene dissembled, clutching at the first excuse that came to mind. "Sorry, we can't make it. I'm, um, showing the Fletcher house to-night."

Claire frowned. She remembered Marty bragging at dinner at the Union Square Grill about how his wife had managed to sell that particular house. "I thought you had sold the Fletcher property."

Marlene was momentarily flustered—a rarity for her. "I . . . I did, but wouldn't you know it, at the last minute the financing fell through. Maybe some other time. Thanks again."

Peyton's culinary masterpiece was a chocolate soufflé, a delicate, extremely rich dish made of egg whites and lush, sweet chocolate whipped into a wispy and ethereal dome.

Once it was in the oven, the sumptuous smell of baking chocolate filled the house. Peyton immediately began cleaning up the kitchen. It seemed as if there was chocolate everywhere.

"It smells great," said Claire.

Peyton grinned mischievously. "I read somewhere that chocolate is a good substitute for sex."

"Well . . . I *like* chocolate," said Claire, "but . . ."

Peyton nodded, but continued to grin impishly. "I guess you and Michael keep those fires burning all the time."

Claire was almost blushing now. "Well, we certainly have always . . . we've always enjoyed each other quite a bit." She paused a moment, troubled suddenly by her husband's recent lack of attention to her. Her worries came flooding back. "But it's been a little different lately. After you have a baby, it's hard." She shrugged. "You're overweight, you're tired, you feel . . . unattractive."

Peyton refused to be convinced. "I'm sure Michael is as attracted to you as the very first day he laid eyes on you. I mean, a man never loses it for his first love."

"Oh, I wasn't Michael's first love. He started too early for me. You want to guess who Michael's first love was, at the tender age of sixteen?"

"Marlene," said Peyton evenly.

Claire's face fell. "How did you know?"

Peyton shrugged lightly. "Wild guess." She bent and peered at the soufflé in the oven. "It's almost ready. It's a shame Michael's going to miss it. What's he working on this late down at the lab anyway?"

"That's a good question," said Claire. Impulsively she picked up the phone in the kitchen and dialed the number of the lab. She listened, scowling as it rang and rang, and had to stop herself from slamming down the phone. "No one answered at the lab."

"Perhaps he's on his way home now."

"Maybe," Claire said uncertainly. "He usually calls when he's leaving."

"I'm sure it's nothing to worry about," said Peyton, laying a reassuring hand on Claire's shoulder.

Michael and Marlene were huddled in a corner of a bar near the lab, busily going over details for the surprise party. Michael had been correct in assuming that Marlene would take over. She had already worked out the menu with the caterer, chosen the wines, and consulted with the florist. All that remained was the guest list, and it looked as if Michael's input was going to be minimal even there.

He sat back in the booth and sipped his drink, then snuck a cigarette. "Got a light?"

Marlene grimaced. "I can't find my Tiffany lighter. Marty's going to throw a fit when he finds out."

Michael lit up and inhaled deeply. "I'm still not sure this whole party thing is a good idea."

Marlene nodded. "Because of Emma?"

Michael tapped his ash. "Because of Emma. And Claire just hasn't been herself lately."

Marlene was silent for a moment, thinking

about what he had just said. "How's Peyton doing?" she asked casually.

Michael smiled warmly. "Oh, Peyton's been terrific."

"Has she?"

He shook his head, as if marveling at his family's immense good luck. "I really don't know what we would have done without her, believe me."

Marlene leaned forward as if she was about to say something, but then caught herself. She was an outspoken woman, but she also knew when not to butt into someone else's business, particularly something as sensitive as this.

She picked up the guest list and scanned it. "Okay," she said, all business suddenly. "Anybody we've missed?"

Claire was in bed reading when Michael came in. He smiled guiltily when he saw her, hating to sneak behind her back, even though his conscience was perfectly clear.

"Hey, sweetheart."

Claire scarcely looked up from her book. "Hi," she said. Her voice was low and gloomy, her greeting unenthusiastic.

Michael started unbuttoning his shirt. "How was your evening?"

"Fine," she replied curtly.

The air in the bedroom seemed to be humming with tension. Wanting to defuse it, he settled on the edge of the bed. "Are you angry with me? I told you I'd be working late, didn't I?"

Claire put down her book and crossed her arms. It was a guarded, defensive gesture, as if she were suddenly wary of her husband.

"I called the lab. No one answered."

Michael was taken by surprise. Lying did not come easy to him. "You called me? Uh . . . I was . . . I must have been in one of the rooms that doesn't have a phone."

Claire was not convinced. "Oh."

"I'm sorry," he said, "I should have called." He slid along the bed and moved to take her in his arms. "I didn't mean to scare you, angel."

She surrendered herself to his arms and then almost immediately pulled back. "Smoke. I smell smoke. Have you been smoking?"

Once again Michael stumbled, ineptly, through the first lie that came to mind. "Uh . . . one of the technicians was smoking. It must be in my hair."

"But you told me once that you never let anyone smoke in the lab," Claire insisted.

Michael was out of lies. Now he *really* wished he had called off the surprise party. Claire was so edgy these days that even a little bit more uncertainty was harmful to her.

"Claire," he said wearily, "I have had a bear of a day, I have been working very hard, and I am very, very tired." He retreated into the bathroom and vigorously brushed his teeth and scrubbed his face, trying to scour the smell of cigarette smoke off of his body.

The strain of the last few weeks, coupled with the confrontation with Claire just before turning in, conspired to give Michael a restless, troubled night's sleep, filled with confused and confusing dreams. During the night he suddenly awoke, bolt upright in the dark bedroom. Something—a noise—had pulled him from his tormented sleep. He could hear a sound he couldn't identify, coming from downstairs.

Michael glanced over at Claire. She was in a deep sleep. He shoved aside the covers and went downstairs, moving silently on the carpeted stairs.

Following the noise to the kitchen, he stopped in the doorway and looked. The only light in the room came from the refrigerator, the door of which was open. Peyton was kneeling on the kitchen floor, picking up pieces of ice that had tumbled from a tray.

She did not seem surprised to see him. Very

slowly she stood up, her eyes never leaving his face, and leaned casually against the refrigerator, the steam of cold air wafting from its freezer compartment. The faint light from the refrigerator revealed the outline of the warm, naked body below the flimsy low-cut negligee she wore.

Her eyes, still on him, were hungry and unwavering.

"I . . . I heard something. A noise," he said.

"I dropped an ice tray. I'm sorry."

Michael turned to go back to bed. "Well, okay. Good night."

"Can I get you something?" she asked quickly.

"What? Oh. No thanks."

Peyton took a step closer to him. "Are you sure?" she whispered, her voice husky. "I could heat something up."

He knew, right then, that he could take her in his arms and kiss her, and for a second he was seized with the desire to do so. But he caught himself. In all his married life he had never been tempted by another woman, not even one as alluring as Peyton.

He stumbled back a step or two. "Thanks anyway," he mumbled. "I better—" He turned and hurried back upstairs, aware of Peyton's eyes on his back.

CHAPTER 17

Emma loved being in charge of things, and on the day of the surprise party Marlene assigned her a very important task. Her job was to get Claire out of the house on a Saturday afternoon and get her back by party time. During the three hours of their absence, Marlene and her squad of caterers would descend on the Bartels' and get the place ready. Guests were due to start arriving at three-thirty and Emma had been told to make sure her mother was back at home as close to four as possible.

Emma had insisted on accompanying her mother on her Saturday-afternoon errands, but as Claire didn't have much more to do than stop at the supermarket and drop off the week's dry cleaning, the child would clearly have her work cut out for her. But then Emma had a brainstorm. She insisted that her mother take her to the Botanical Gardens, knowing that Claire wouldn't be able to tear herself away.

Emma contented herself playing among the greenhouses, but never ignored her very important job. She ran up to her mother, who was still fretting over her orchids.

"Mommy, what time is it?"

Claire looked at her watch. "It's almost four o'clock."

"Perfect," said Emma. "I mean—" She faked a yawn. "I'm tired. Let's go home."

Claire turned back to her plant, misting it gently. "In a minute, honey."

Emma did not hesitate. She grabbed her mother by the hand and started pulling her toward the exit. "Mommy, come on."

Claire sighed, resigned. Emma had been a good, patient girl all afternoon. It really was time to go.

In the car Emma seemed more bright-eyed than usual, not in the slightest bit tired. "Don't forget to stop at the cleaners," she told her mother.

"I thought you were beat."

"Peyton told me to remind you."

Claire started the engine of the Volvo wagon. "Okay, my little coordinator."

The dry cleaners was only a few blocks from the Botanical Gardens and Emma stayed in the car while Claire dashed in with an armload of clothing.

Jerry, the cleaner, greeted her by name. "How you doing, Mrs. Bartel? Where's Emma?"

Claire dumped the clothing on the counter. "She's in the car."

Jerry readied his pad and was pawing through the clothes. "Bring her in next time. . . . Let's see. Four pants. Two—no, three shirts. Light starch, right?"

Claire handed over the blue blazer. "This jacket reeks of cigarette smoke."

Jerry looked faintly surprised as he took the garment and patted the pockets. "I didn't know your husband was a smoker."

"He isn't. I mean, he hasn't been for a long time. He quit when we got married."

"Well, we'll get the smell out of this, don't you worry." Jerry's hand rooted about in the side pocket of the blue blazer. "What's this?"

Marlene's gold lighter glittered in his palm. "Mrs. Bartel, I hate to be the one to tell you, but it looks like your husband's got a habit he's been hiding from you."

Claire picked up the lighter and stared at it.

"MC" was engraved in the soft, smooth gold—there was no doubt that the lighter belonged to Marlene. In a sudden, asphyxiating rush she knew that all of her worst fears had been confirmed. Her eyes widened, her knees felt weak, and her stomach churned. She felt her chest grow tight.

"Are you all right?" asked Jerry. "Mrs. Bartel? Mrs. Bartel—"

She ran out of the dry cleaners and got in the car, gasping, the asthmatic wheeze rising in her throat.

"Mommy, what's wrong?"

"Nothing, honey, nothing . . ." Claire pulled the inhaler out of the glove compartment and shot some of her medicine into her lungs. She slumped over the wheel until she was sure she could drive safely. Then she put the car in gear and got home as quickly as she could.

Emma tugged at her hand, leading her into the kitchen, then attempting to guide her to the living room. The house was silent and seemed deserted.

Claire disengaged herself from her daughter's clutching hands and pulled out a kitchen chair. She was not sure her legs would support her. She hunched over the table and rubbed her throbbing temples.

"Mom," Emma cajoled, "what are you doing? Let's go inside. I want you to come inside."

"Emma," Claire said as steadily as she could, "I want you to go up to your room and play for a while."

"But, *Mom*!"

"Emma," Claire snapped, "I need a moment."

Emma could see that her mother was terribly upset and it frightened her. She dashed further into the house.

Claire's brain reeled, a sickening dizziness sweeping over her. The world—her world—which had once seemed so happy, so complete, was now in ruins. She felt loathing and hate, an unconscious self-pity, a deep guilt, and a revolting sense of sexual betrayal. Everything—and everyone—she held dear had double-crossed her. Even her son would not take her breast. And now her husband and her closest friend had conspired to deceive her. Her home, her friendship, and her marriage had been violated. She felt as if she had been beaten down by those she trusted and thought she loved. For a moment she thought she was going to lose her mind.

Then Michael entered the room, calm and solicitous as he always was. Steady, firm, reliable Michael. The Michael other women coveted, the man who had fathered her children and who had sworn to be with her for life. But now she saw him for what he really was: a fake, a fraud, and a hypocrite.

"Claire," he asked, "what's the matter?"

Her eyes were as cold as her voice. "How could you do this to me?"

"What do you mean?"

"You know damn well, you son of a bitch!" Her voice spiraled into a loud screech.

Michael winced and glanced uneasily into the other room. "Claire, *please*."

"Don't you 'Claire please' me," she spat, throwing down the gold lighter like a gambler playing a trump card. "You have been lying to me."

"Calm down," Michael pleaded. "Please . . ."

Claire's anger flashed. "Goddammit! Don't tell me to calm down!"

"Claire," Michael implored. "You don't understand."

"Oh, I understand," she shot back. "Sure I do."

"No, you don't," he insisted.

Claire filled her lungs and shouted. "You've been fucking Marlene!"

"Enough! Enough! There are people inside. There are people waiting here to see you. Your friends. Our friends."

"What are you talking about?"

"This." Michael grabbed her by the arm and marched her into the living room.

There, gathered like people posing for a group photograph, were all of their friends and neighbors, people from the lab, her coworkers from the Botanical Gardens. Emma stood in the foreground, Peyton's arms draped over her shoulders.

Marlene's eyes seemed to blaze, searing her. She looked at Claire for a moment, then grabbed her purse and stalked to the front door.

Marty held a platter bearing a giant white-and-green cake, shaped like a greenhouse. Raising it apologetically, he said, "Surprise."

CHAPTER 18

The party went ahead, awkward and strained and, to no one's surprise, ended early. Claire sleepwalked through the celebration, numb with shock and embarrassment. But beneath her humiliation lurked a deeper worry.

It was the sense that something had gone very wrong with her life, that it was weak at its very foundation. Something had brought her to this state, some unseen malevolent force had made her mistrust her husband and her friends, made her see enemies everywhere.

The only way she could cope with it was by shutting down, trying to remove herself from the scene. After the last guest had left, she went around the house as if nothing untoward had happened, clearing plates, stacking glasses, and wrapping leftovers. Emma was nowhere to be seen, and even Peyton, who would normally have come forward to console and assist, stayed out of sight.

She was scraping dishes in the kitchen when Michael came in and stood behind her. She could feel the silent challenge of his presence like a heavy weight.

"Well," she said briskly, "it wasn't a complete disaster."

"Complete disaster?" Michael said sarcastically. "No, it wasn't a complete disaster. No one got killed, if that's what you mean."

Claire's shoulders slumped. "I really appreciate your going to the trouble of throwing me the party. It was a . . . very nice thought."

Michael's anger sparked. "I don't give a damn about the party. I care about *you*. Where's your trust? Where's the old Claire?" He turned from her, disgusted.

"Michael . . ." He walked out of the kitchen. "Don't walk away from me! Michael! Please . . ."

That night they slept in separate rooms, both of them restless and tormented by the fears and anxieties of families in danger of unraveling.

The next morning, Claire and Michael met on the closest thing to neutral ground in their house. They met in Joe's nursery.

"Have you spoken to Marlene yet?" he asked.

"I—I don't know how I can face her." Claire laid Joe in his crib and then turned toward her husband. "Michael, come back to our bed tonight. I can't say I'm sorry more than I have already." She slipped her arms around him. "I can't sleep without you."

He smoothed her hair tenderly. "Okay, honey. Okay . . ."

"I've been thinking. Maybe we could get away together. Even if it's only for a few days."

Michael nodded. "That's a good idea. I think I could get some time off. Are you talking about Peyton and the kids or just us?"

"I was thinking just the family. Without Peyton . . ." Her voice trailed off, as if she was afraid of discussing Peyton with her husband.

"I don't get it. I thought you liked having Peyton around."

"I do and I don't."

"Claire, if you don't like the way Peyton's doing something, why don't you just tell her?"

"It's more complicated than that," Claire said plaintively. "Much more."

"You sound like you're turning on Peyton."

"I'm not turning on her. That makes it sound like I have a grudge against her. It's just that . . . so many things have gone wrong since she arrived."

"You *can't* be saying those things have been Peyton's fault, are you?"

"No . . . I don't know. Maybe it was a mistake hiring a live-in nanny in the first place."

"Peyton has come through for this family in some very difficult times, Claire."

Downstairs in the kitchen, Peyton sat stock-still at the table, her blood racing.

"Please let's just get away together," Claire pleaded. "We can talk about it then."

Michael gave in. "Okay," he said. "We'll go away, just the family. Will that make you happy?"

"Yes."

Downstairs, Peyton turned her wide, mad eyes to the side and looked down at the baby intercom, standing on the kitchen table.

The clock radio next to Peyton's bed clicked on, and classical music began playing softly in the dark. She awoke immediately and snapped it off. It was three o'clock in the morning.

She slipped out of bed and pulled on a pair of blue jeans and a loose sweater, then silently made her way through the sleeping house and out to the greenhouse. She opened the door and felt her way to the mechanism that controlled the roof windows. Claire had oiled the gears and the brake until it worked perfectly. Very carefully Peyton slipped off the catch and cranked the windows open; then holding them ajar, she put her weight on the chain and disconnected the safety brake. Finally she jammed a shovel into the gear and stepped back. The whole apparatus rested precariously on the shaft of the shovel. The blade was within the arc of the door, acting as a trigger. If the shovel was knocked away, the windows would smash closed.

Peyton closed the door of the greenhouse behind her, the apparatus within kept open by the precarious pressure of the shovel alone, like a trap ready to snap shut.

CHAPTER 19

Marlene was tough. She had a temper that would burn as hot as a volcano and she could definitely bear a grudge if she chose to, but she cared about the people she loved. She was still angry with Claire, angry that Claire had allowed her jealousy to overcome her good sense, angry that she could even have suspected her best friend of attempting to steal her husband, angry that she hadn't trusted more. But the resentment wasn't deep. Give it a couple of days to blow over, a week or two for the embarrassment, and then things would go back to normal, more or less.

In the meantime Marlene had a business to run. She hadn't become one of Seattle's most high-powered real-estate agents by being thin-skinned. She was at her desk by eight in the morning no matter how late she had been out the night before, and she never left her office until every bit of the day's business had been accomplished.

She was blessed with the ability to do several tasks at once. She could read her mail and dictate letters, make notes and crunch numbers on her personal computer at the same time. She had an assistant fifteen years younger than she was and she could outwork him without breaking a sweat. Burnout was the primary cause of employee turnover at her office.

At the moment she was dictating a blue streak, pausing only to drag on her cigarette, while casting her eyes over the business pages of that morning's paper. She held the dicta-phone microphone close to her mouth, as if she was on the verge of taking a bite out of it.

"And if there are any further services that I or my staff might provide, please do not hesi-tate to call blah, blah, blah."

She sucked on her cigarette and prepared to dictate her next letter. There was a knock at the door and one of her assistants, a bright-eyed, Ivy League–looking young man, came into her office.

"Marlene, the new listing notices have just

come in." He put a sheaf of papers and photographs down on her wide desk.

New listings were the raw material of real estate. She grabbed the papers and flipped through them. "Most of these are old. Yeah, I've seen these before . . . the Rosen house, the Pentel house. Dogs. These aren't going to sell until the market firms up." She had an encyclopedic knowledge of every high-end residential property for sale in the greater Seattle area.

"No, nothing here for us . . ." she continued, then paused, a large glossy color photograph in her hand.

"Found something?" her assistant asked.

The photograph depicted a large antiseptic-looking hilltop mansion in Newport Shores in Bellevue that commanded a sweeping view of the lake.

"Well, I'll be damned," she said. "Dr. Victor Mott. The good doctor's property is still on the market." She squinted at the photograph for a moment, then opened a drawer in her desk and pulled out a magnifying glass. She examined the picture closely, a little jolt of surprise shooting through her.

"Look at that."

"What?" asked her assistant.

Marlene looked up. "You still here? What are you waiting for? A tip?"

The young man could tell when he wasn't wanted. He scurried from the room.

Marlene returned to the photograph and smiled to herself. Hanging from a window in the house once occupied by Victor and Peyton Mott was a set of wind chimes identical to the one now hanging from the window of the Bartel nursery. Marlene picked up a heavy black grease pencil and circled that minute detail.

Then she stood, crushed out her cigarette, and shrugged on her suit jacket.

"I'm going to the library. Cancel the rest of my morning," she ordered as she walked briskly for the door.

Her assistant looked alarmed. "The library! But you have the Rauch meeting at eleven and a closing with the Richardsons at twelve-fifteen!"

Marlene tossed an angry look over her shoulder. "So?"

"Well, what should I tell them?" the young man asked.

The look she gave him would have withered a houseplant. "Make something up," she snapped. "You've got a Harvard education."

In her little Mercedes sports car Marlene zoomed down the highway toward the Kings County Library as if she were the only person on the road. She pulled into the parking lot next to the low, red-brick building and screeched to a halt.

Inside the library she commandeered the services of a librarian, rapping out orders like a field marshal. In a matter of minutes she was set up with a microfilm reader and the last year's worth of *Seattle Examiner*s. She even got the librarian to thread the tape into the reader for her—no one argued with Marlene when she was at her bossiest.

It took about an hour, but when she found what she was looking for, she sat back in the hard library chair and stared at the image on the screen, a self-satisfied smirk on her face. Absentmindedly she reached for a cigarette and then remembered she was in a library.

On the microfilm reader was a grainy black-and-white picture, a crowd of mourners at the funeral of Dr. Victor Mott. Front and center, in the place of honor, was a picture of the grieving widow. She was dressed from head to toe in black, but even in the poorly reproduced photograph it was plain that she was heavily pregnant. And behind her big dark glasses it was obvious who she was—Peyton.

"No doubt about it," Marlene whispered.

She hurried out of the library without even bothering to rewind the tape and return it to the desk.

She burned rubber as she drove out of the library parking lot, steering with one hand and using the other to punch the Bartels' number into the keypad of her car phone. She flipped on the speaker and waited impatiently as the phone rang.

"Hello?" The voice was Peyton's.

Marlene's lips formed themselves into a sneer. "Let me talk to Claire," she said icily. She gunned her car through a yellow light, narrowly missing a pedestrian.

"May I ask who's calling?" said Peyton. Something in Marlene's voice worried her and she was stalling her. She could sense Marlene's urgency.

Marlene laughed harshly. "Yeah, you can ask who's calling. Marlene Craven. You want me to spell it?"

"Claire's not here," said Peyton.

"Of course she isn't."

"I'll tell her you called."

"Oh, *sure* you will." Marlene broke the connection, swerved around a column of slow-moving traffic, and quickly tapped out another number.

"Biotechniques."

"Let me talk to Dr. Michael Bartel."

"One moment." As the switchboard operator at Michael's lab put her on hold, light classical music began to play. The delicate harmonies did nothing to soothe Marlene's tightly wound spirit.

The cool voice of the receptionist came back on the line. "I'm sorry. He's not in his office and he's not answering his page."

Marlene expressed her displeasure at this piece of unwelcome news in a few choice obscenities.

"May I take a message?" the receptionist asked calmly.

"Yes. Tell him to call Marlene Craven the minute he's free. It's very important."

She had no luck at the Botanical Gardens either. The switchboard there told her that Claire had been in the greenhouses and might still be, but if she was, she would be in the potting shed, putting away her tools after her shift.

"Well, then put me through to the potting shed," she snapped.

"There is no phone in the potting shed," came the reply.

Marlene rolled her eyes. How could anyone be unreachable by telephone? Between her car phone, her beeper, and the seven extensions in her house, Marlene could be tracked down anytime day or night.

"But she *might* be on her way home?"

"That's right, ma'am. She was supposed to be here between nine and twelve today."

"Well, if she hasn't left, tell her that Marlene called and she has to call me back. It's urgent!"

"Yes, ma'am."

Marlene tooled through the streets, wondering what she should do next. The information she had uncovered both thrilled and appalled her and she burned to tell someone. She also ached to confront Peyton—and to find out exactly what the alleged nanny was up to. Of course, she was sure of one thing: Dr. Victor Mott's widow was not working at the Bartels' out of the goodness of her heart.

Marlene remembered the troubles that Claire and Michael had faced in the last few weeks—the missing report, the dismissal of Solomon, the surprise-party fiasco, Claire's suspicions of Michael—and thought that somehow they were all Peyton's fault, the working of some kind of twisted revenge against the woman who had blown the whistle on her pervert husband. And Marlene would have bet her next ten commissions that Peyton was not done yet, that she would not stop until she had completely destroyed her enemies.

Suddenly, with a flash of apprehension, Marlene realized that Peyton was at home, alone with baby Joe. She couldn't imagine any woman, even Peyton, hurting an innocent infant, but she decided to get over to the Bartel house and wait until Claire got home. They would confront Peyton together.

She stamped down hard on the gas pedal and leaned on the horn. A minivan was in the middle of an intersection waiting to make a left turn. The cars behind it were lined up, their drivers waiting patiently.

Not Marlene. She tapped the wheel impatiently and lit a cigarette. "Are you kidding me? You're kidding me, right." She saw a break in the traffic. "Go! Go!" The van waited until the road was absolutely clear.

"What is this? A parade?" She had enough of waiting. She floored the gas pedal and cut around the cars in front of her and the cautious minivan driver, zooming through the intersection.

Marlene was smiling to herself as she drove up the hill into Madison Park, happy that she had finally nailed Peyton. She hadn't liked her from the beginning. There was nothing quite as satisfying as being proved right. She was actually looking forward to confronting the so-called nanny, to throwing her out of the Bartel house, to getting her hand *off* the cradle.

* * *

The messages Marlene had scattered around town were beginning to get through. Michael returned to the office to the news that Marlene had called, but he was just about to go into a meeting and couldn't return her call. Still, the news pleased him. Maybe things were going to be getting back to normal.

Claire was leaving the potting shed when she got her message. She read it and then stuffed it in the pocket of her blue jeans. She would call Marlene the minute she got home.

Peyton was gently swaying back and forth in the wicker rocker in the nursery, Joe draped over her shoulder. She was thinking about Marlene and the phone call. If Marlene had discovered anything, she would have to be dealt with. It was as simple as that.

Joe started wriggling and gurgling. Peyton lifted him, holding him at arm's length high above her face.

"Oooooh," she cooed. "Mommy loves you so much, my sweet little pumpkin."

Joe laughed and squirmed and kicked his legs in delight.

The doorbell chimed. Quickly she put Joe down in his crib, then hurried down the stairs. She was not surprised to see Marlene standing on the steps. The instant the door was opened, Marlene pushed by Peyton into the house.

"Claire! It's Marlene! Claire, where are you?"

Peyton decided that she would try the innocent act. "Marlene, are you all right?"

Marlene turned and glared at her. "No," she said scornfully, "I need a doctor. Know of any, Mrs. Mott?"

"You know?"

Marlene nodded curtly. "I know. Where is she?"

Peyton bowed her head, as if submitting to the inevitable. "She's in the greenhouse," she said.

"Good." Marlene stormed triumphantly through the living room and out the backdoor.

"Claire?" she called as she ran down the porch steps.

Marlene stopped outside the closed greenhouse door. "Claire, are you in there? This is important. It has nothing to do with the party." She shoved the door open and stepped inside.

The edge of the door smacked into the shovel, knocking it away from the chain and wheel. In a split second the line rattled through the mechanism, the wheel spinning. The windows in the roof of the greenhouse smashed shut. Marlene looked up into a shower of sharp glass hurtling toward her.

She had time to scream and to throw up her thin, manicured hands to protect herself from the deadly downpour. The first fragments of glass sliced into her hands and face like daggers. Slivers peppered her skin, laying open a gash on her face to the cheekbone. Blood gushed from the deep wound, drenching her chest and neck. Two more lethal darts pierced her, one driving deep into her neck, the other stabbing easily through her clothes and deep into her chest.

She fell to the brickwork floor of the greenhouse, choking on her own blood, unable to cry for help. Pain and panic enveloped her as she flailed, trying to hang on to life.

Peyton stood on the porch, listening to the death convulsions of her enemy. In a matter of moments Marlene ceased to struggle.

When all was silent, Peyton walked calmly into the house. In the kitchen she opened a drawer and removed an inhaler. Methodically she pumped it until it was empty and then put it back. There were other such devices scattered around the house—in the study, in the family room, in the bathroom off the master bedroom, in the bedside table. It took only minutes to empty them all.

Then she dressed Joe warmly, put him in his stroller, and took him for an outing in the park.

* * *

Claire was slightly apprehensive when she saw Marlene's Mercedes parked in the driveway. First the message at work; now she had come to the house. Maybe Marlene was ready to talk things over. Whatever happened, though, Claire hoped there would be no scene. She couldn't cope with that now.

Claire slung her purse over her shoulder, took a tray of seedlings from the back of the Volvo station wagon, and circled around the back to the greenhouse. As if to calm herself before entering the main house, she wanted to put away her precious plants.

She pushed open the door of the greenhouse and stepped inside, glass crunching under her feet. Marlene lay sprawled in a pool of her own blood, her eyes open and staring, as if startled by the violence of her end.

"Oh, my God!" Claire screamed. The seedlings fell with a crash, and she dropped her purse. She staggered backward out of the greenhouse, then ran for the house.

The onset of the asthma attack was almost immediate, easily the most severe one she had ever had. By the time she reached the porch steps, she was desperately wheezing. She stumbled into the kitchen and snatched at the phone, her numb and trembling hands unable to hold the receiver. Finally she was able to dial emergency.

Her ears filled with the sounds of her struggle for breath, she heard the voice say, "Nine-one-one. The nature of your emergency?"

Claire's tormented voice was lost in wheezing. Her lips worked and her mouth opened and shut, but she couldn't form the words. An all-encompassing hysteria closed around her like a vise, crushing her.

The emergency-services operator was still on the line, listening to the agonized breathing. "Hello? Hello?" The operator hit the trace button on her console.

Claire did her best to think clearly. She tore open the kitchen drawer, sending knives and forks and spoons tumbling to the floor, dove for the inhaler, and fired it into her mouth. Her eyes grew wide and her panic redoubled as she realized it was empty.

She stumbled up the stairs and swept open the drawer in the night table. She seized the inhaler and put it to her mouth. It, too, was empty.

She almost tore the bathroom medicine cabinet off its hinges, then scrabbled through the containers and tubes. A bottle of mouthwash hit the porcelain sink and exploded, filling the room with a cloying, minty smell. She shot the inhaler into her mouth. Empty . . .

Only one inhaler remained. She knew it was full; she had bought it only the day before. It was in her purse. And her purse was in the greenhouse.

Dizzy from lack of oxygen, Claire tottered down the stairs and staggered through the wreckage of the kitchen to the porch.

She could just about make out her purse lying wedged in the doorway of the greenhouse and started toward it, one painful step after another. Then the ground seemed to rush up to meet her. Suddenly she was lying on the porch, her eyes wide.

Then a great, crushing blackness overwhelmed her.

CHAPTER 20

Consciousness came back to Claire in stages. First she recognized that she *was* aware, that the blackness was receding, as if a heavy curtain were being drawn back from the window. Then she began to hear a mélange of noises that she could not at first separate into their component parts. Gradually they became voices, some near, some far, some seeming to issue from a loudspeaker. In the background she recognized the thrum of rain, beating down steadily on a windowsill.

Her eyes fluttered open to a confused mix of colors and shapes, light and dark. She blinked several times, and the scene before her settled into a recognizable pattern.

Michael's face, a picture of concern, appeared. "Are you awake, Claire? Can you hear me?"

Claire nodded.

Michael stroked her forehead gently. "Everything is okay, honey. You're safe in a hospital."

"Hospital?"

"Don't worry. You're going to be all right."

Her mind grappled with the words she had just heard. Why was she in a hospital? She was fine. . . . Then, in a horrifying blitz of memories, it all came back to her. The panic, the fear, the crippling asthma attack . . . Marlene. Lying in the greenhouse. Her blood . . . And her unseeing eyes.

Claire tried to sit up. Her brain commanded her muscles to work, but they refused to obey her. Michael shushed her and gently pushed her back down on the bed.

Claire's voice was barely audible. "Marlene . . . ?"

Michael's expression changed. He looked away from his wife. "It was an accident, Claire. You can't blame yourself."

Her hand reached out and clutched at his arm, her eyes wild with alarm. "Marlene . . ." Tears started to course down her cheeks.

"I know how hard it is, sweetheart," he said sadly. "Please try to rest." He tried his best to comfort her, stroking her hand until she fell asleep.

Michael rose stiffly to his feet and walked out of the room. Peyton and Emma were waiting for him in the corridor, Emma in Peyton's lap. Joe was asleep in his stroller. The little girl's face was streaked with tears and Peyton's expression was the very image of grave concern.

Michael scooped his daughter up in his arms.

"How's Mommy?" she asked, clinging to him.

He stroked her hair. "Mommy's going to have to stay here for a little while longer, but she's going to be just fine. Don't worry about it, honey."

Peyton looked relieved. "Thank God." She raised her eyes heavenward. Silently she cursed the circumstances that had allowed Claire to escape death. If the emergency-services operator had not had the presence of mind to trace the call and send out the paramedics, Claire would have been dead by now.

"C'mon," said Michael. "Let's go home."

He led the way out of the hospital, Emma in his arms. Peyton followed, pushing the stroller. Instinctively Michael paused at the entrance to gather his family together before ushering them out into the wet, cold night.

The admitting nurse at the reception desk

watched them, thinking to herself that they were a lovely-looking family.

Michael was so anxious to get his children out of the rain that he did not look right or left as he rushed across the parking lot to their car. None of them noticed a figure standing in the shrubbery that ringed the parking lot.

Huddled in the cold and wet was Solomon, his red bike at his side. He had laboriously read the short item in the newspaper about Marlene's death and Claire's collapse. He found it hard to comprehend the exact details but had realized the most important fact. Claire had been hurt, his family was in trouble.

He looked up at the lighted windows of the hospital, wondering which room belonged to Claire. Then he put his hands together and prayed.

The soaking rain continued all night. Toward midnight, the inky black of the sky cracked with a flash of bright white lightning.

The weather did not disturb Peyton in the least. She had hummed to herself as she tidied the house, fed her family, and put Emma to bed. It was her first night without Claire in the house, and she was enjoying it immensely. Soon it would be like this permanently.

The obstacles in her path were vanishing. Marlene was gone for good, Claire for the moment—but there would be other chances in the future. And when she was gone, the grieving Michael and Emma would fall into her, Peyton's, arms. By the time Joe was old enough to know, Claire would hardly be a dim memory.

Still singing to herself, Peyton went into the nursery and picked up Joe. He was sleepy and limp in her arms and she rocked him gently and sang softly.

"Hush little baby, don't say a word, Mama's going to buy you a mockingbird." She held him close, resting her chin lightly on the soft hair on his head. "And if that mockingbird don't sing, Mama's going to buy you a diamond ring. . . ."

Joe's sleep-heavy eyes closed and he sighed drowsily. Peyton put him down in the crib.

The thunder rumbled and the rain beat down, but beneath the storm there was another sound, the sound of hammering. Peyton glanced out the window into the yard.

Michael was standing before the greenhouse, angrily pounding nails into two stout boards across the doorway. He was soaked to the skin, but seemed oblivious to the water pouring down his face as he struck at the nails furiously, taking out his rage on the frail structure.

Pausing only to put on a jacket, Peyton hurried out to him and tried to lead him back inside.

"Michael," she pleaded. "Please . . ."

He looked at her, but didn't seem to see her. "I keep seeing Marlene's face," he said, his voice shot through with anguish. He shook his head, water streaming from his hair. "I just can't believe she's gone."

Peyton put her arm around his shoulder and guided him back to the house as if assisting an invalid. The kitchen, lit only by a single red-shaded lamp on the antique farmhouse table, was warm and comforting.

"You have to get those wet things off," said Peyton. "You can't get sick, too."

He did not protest as she unbuttoned his shirt and stripped it from him, and he said nothing when she picked up a towel and started to dry his naked back and shoulders. Her movements were slow, warm and languid. Michael closed his eyes and breathed out heavily. . . .

"You're soaked through," Peyton said, her voice velvety and seductive. She moved around to face him, gently moving the towel across his ribs and nipples, as if teasing them. "Soaked through . . ." Her voice trailed off.

Their eyes were locked together. She moved to dry his face, never taking her gaze from his.

A drop of water from her own wet hair slipped down her cheek to her lips. She licked it off as if it were tinged with honey.

"Peyton," Michael said in a hoarse whisper. "You must stop this."

"Sssh." The towel moved into his hair, caressing his head.

"I've never been unfaithful."

Peyton nodded. "I know."

"There is only one woman for me."

Peyton leaned in close to him, her lips almost on his ear, as if about to kiss him. "I know. All you need is one woman."

Gently she pulled away from him and draped the towel around his neck.

"Good night," she said softly.

CHAPTER 21

Claire's body mended more quickly than her spirit. The hospital, with its antiseptic air, the false cheerfulness of the nurses, and the brisk, impersonal ministrations of the doctors, depressed her.

Nothing in the hospital, however, made her as despondent as the thoughts of what had put her there. She felt betrayed by her own body. If she had been able to breathe like a normal person, she would have made the simple phone call, summoned an ambulance, and saved her friend. Claire was tormented by her last sight of Marlene and the look of anger and shocked betrayal in her sightless eyes.

Michael, who faithfully visited her twice a

day, assured her that there was nothing she could have done, that the phone call would not have made any difference.

He could not bring himself to say the word "dead." By the time Claire arrived on the scene, she was "already gone," he said, as if Marlene had left on a long journey. "There was nothing you could do. She was already gone."

"And Marty?" she asked.

"He's gone back east to stay with his family for a while."

That was not what she meant. "Does he blame me?"

"Of course not!" Michael said firmly, but his eyes betrayed him, and he knew it. He looked away.

Guilt and sorrow were with her from the moment she awoke in her hospital bed in the morning to the time she fell into an uneasy sleep at night. They were even with her when she asked about Joe and Emma, hungry for news of her children. She never mentioned Peyton.

Claire was released from the hospital ten days after she was admitted. As Michael and Emma wheeled her out of the building into the bright sunlight in the parking lot, her spirits lifted.

"It's good to be outside," she remarked.

"You can go to the Botanical Gardens tomorrow," said Michael, helping her out of the wheelchair at the car door.

"I don't know why I need this thing," Claire said. "I can walk perfectly well."

"It's just a hospital regulation."

She settled in the front passenger seat. Emma was in the back. Michael started the engine.

"How are you doing, honey?" He was being overly solicitous, acting as if Claire were elderly or disabled.

"Fine."

"Got your medication?"

"In my purse," she said. "I'll have to stop by the pharmacy tomorrow."

"I'll go," he said quickly.

"I'll manage."

As the car moved out of the lot Emma squirmed around and looked out the back window just as Solomon emerged from the bushes on his bicycle and pedaled furiously after them. He had kept up his vigil for the full ten days of Claire's confinement, rushing down to the hospital every time he had a free minute. His perseverance had paid off. His smile flashed and Emma waved, hoping that her parents didn't see.

"Emma," said Claire. *"Emma."*

Emma turned to face the front of the car. "Yes?"

"Put on your seat belt."

Emma buckled herself in, then managed one last quick glance out the rear window of the car. The Volvo had lost Solomon somewhere back there in traffic.

"Everything all right, sweetheart?" Claire asked.

Emma was annoyed to have lost sight of her friend. "Yes," she said irritably.

When the car pulled up in front of the house, Claire looked at the familiar building through different eyes, as if seeing something she had never noticed before. It was her home, but it seemed considerably less welcoming than it ever had before.

It was different inside, too. Someone else had cleaned it, someone else had polished the furniture, and someone else was cooking dinner in the kitchen.

As Claire stood in the hall and looked around, Michael bustled in behind her, carrying her small suitcase. Everything was in its accustomed place, as it had always been, yet everything was somehow different.

Peyton appeared from the kitchen. She was simply dressed, but perfectly put together, her hair combed and her slacks pressed to a sharp crease. The color and life in her cheeks and eyes contrasted with Claire's pallor. She seemed to radiate health and happiness.

She kissed Claire on the cheek, her lips as smooth and as cold as porcelain. "Hello, Claire! It's so good to have you home."

"It's good to be home," Claire said.

"Here," said Michael, "I'll take your purse upstairs for you."

Claire clutched the pocketbook to her chest. "I'm not an invalid, Michael."

"Oh," said Peyton, turning businesslike for a moment. "Before I forget, Michael, the secretary of the school board called back. She said the meeting is next Thursday night. I put it in your book for you."

"Thanks, Peyton." He could feel Claire's inquiring look. "It's a fundraiser. Peyton heard about it when she picked Emma up at school."

"Oh." Claire's gaze traveled to Peyton's wrist. Her own gold-and-garnet bracelet, a gift from Michael, dangled from her arm.

Peyton followed her gaze. "You said I should borrow it. Is it all right?"

A series of interconnected thoughts streaked through Claire's brain. If Peyton was wearing the bracelet, she had been in her bedroom, rummaging among her belongings.

"I'm sorry," said Peyton, her face clouding. "I hope I haven't done anything wrong."

"It's fine," said Claire evenly.

The nanny smiled cheerfully, the crisis past. "I have to get back to the kitchen. I want to make sure I don't burn dinner." She ducked back into the kitchen.

Claire turned on her heel and made for the stairs. She wanted to see her son. Michael followed, as if afraid to let her out of his sight.

Joe was sleeping soundly in his crib and Claire felt a great warm rush of love for him. She smiled and tears gathered in the corners of her eyes. This was the kind of therapy she needed. One little sleepy smile from Joe was all it would take to mend her soul.

"Hello, honey," she whispered. She bent and reached into the crib to wake him.

Michael stopped her. "Don't do that."

"Why not?"

"Peyton said not to wake him. He had a very fussy night."

"Oh? And where were you?"

Michael seemed puzzled by the question. "Where was I?"

"When our son was having a fussy night?"

"I was asleep."

"I see." She straightened. Her eyes caught sight of the wallpaper. Carefully painted around the top of the walls in lush greens and blues was a frieze of turtles. "What's with the wallpaper?"

Michael smiled. "Peyton did it. Don't you like it?"

"It would have been nice if someone had thought to ask me first," she said, irritated.

"We thought it could be a surprise, Claire. We thought you'd like it. I'll have her take it down if you like."

Claire shrugged. "It doesn't matter. I think I'll lie down for a while."

"You do that," he said, and left the room quickly, as if making his escape.

Claire was finding it hard to lie still. She was haunted by the events of the last ten days and couldn't shake the disconcerting sense that she was a guest in her own house.

She swung out of bed and, for want of something better to do, started unpacking her suitcase, sorting the few clothes into piles for the laundry. Folded neatly in the bottom of the case were the blue jeans she had been wearing that terrible day. Checking the pockets, she found the crumpled piece of paper she had been given at the Botanical Gardens that day.

Call Marlene Craven, it read, *urgent*. The last word was underlined twice. What, Claire thought, could have been so urgent? She knew

Marlene well; there was little chance that she *urgently* needed to explain the misunderstandings of the surprise party. It must have been something else. Tomorrow, Claire decided, she would find out.

CHAPTER 22

The staff at Marlene's real-estate office was a little wary of Claire when she arrived the next morning. It hadn't taken long for the gossip about the surprise-party fiasco to make the rounds, and everybody knew the circumstances of Marlene's horrible death in Claire's greenhouse. Everybody called it an accident, but Marlene's staff was distrustful and suspicious of Claire nonetheless.

"But *why* do you want to see her office?" her assistant asked.

Claire herself didn't know, not exactly. She just had a feeling that Marlene's death was more than a simple, tragic accident.

She took out the piece of paper she had found

in her jeans pocket last night. "I got this message the day she died," she said, showing him the note. "You knew her. If Marlene said it was urgent, then it was *urgent*."

"Yeah," the young man said dubiously, "but how will we ever know what it was?"

"That's what I'm here to find out," said Claire.

Marlene's office had been untouched since she died, everything remaining on her desk as if it were a shrine. Claire examined the objects, the few framed photos—there was one of Marty and one of Claire and Michael and Emma taken when they had all gone skiing together in Squaw Valley.

The assistant lingered near the desk, as if afraid that Claire would defile something.

"What did she do that morning?" she asked.

"Well . . . She was here when I came in—she always was. Everything was normal until about ten-thirty or eleven that morning. She came out of her office all of a sudden and told me to cancel her entire morning. A big meeting and a closing. That wasn't like her. Business always came first with Marlene."

Claire nodded. "I know. Did she say what was up? Did she say where she was going in such a hurry?"

The young man shrugged. "She said she was going to the library."

"The library?"

"Yeah, strange, isn't it?"

"Did she say what she was looking for? Was it business-related? A title search, maybe?"

He shook his head. "No, Marlene didn't do drudge work like that. We have researchers that do that kind of thing. She said she was going to the library—she just didn't say why. I'm sorry."

Claire thought for a moment. "What was Marlene doing right before she went to the library?"

The assistant thought, his brow furrowed. "I had just given her the new listings. She looked at them, then she kicked me out. About ten minutes later she took off like a bat out of hell."

"Are the listings here on the desk?"

The assistant nodded and tapped a pile of papers. "Right here."

Claire took the sheaf of papers and looked at them carefully. They meant very little to her until she saw the Mott house. She held the photo close to her face and saw, with a jolt of horror, the wind chimes circled heavily in black.

Her hand went to her mouth. "Oh, my God . . ." she gasped.

"What is it?"

Claire shook her head. "It's nothing. I mean— I have to go."

Claire brought her car to a halt outside the Mott house and looked at it for a moment, listening to the gentle tinkling of the wind chimes dangling from one of the gutters. She felt a cold fear run through her, as if this modern white house were an evil and forbidding fairy-tale castle.

She got out of the car and walked around the building, unsure of what to do next. She stood on the sidewalk for a moment, then, just as she turned to get back in her car, the wide front door of the house swung open and a man came out.

"Mrs. Boyajian! At last we meet." The man was walking toward her quickly, his hand out, a big salesman's smile on his face. "Bruce Silverman, from Carney Realty. I was afraid you were going to stand me up." He pumped her hand.

"I'm sorry, I'm not—I was just—"

"No, no, don't apologize. Better late than never. Let's take a look inside, shall we?" He ushered her through the front door. "I think you're going to love this place. It's one of the best houses on the market in this range. Thirty-two hundred square feet, designer everything,

Euro-style kitchen. They spared no expense on this baby."

The house was furnished, but it had a cold, sterile, unlived-in air. The furniture was modern, chrome and glass and leather, the floors marble. Claire recognized the style; it was the same sterile elegance she had seen in Dr. Victor Mott's office on that terrible day all those months ago.

She walked from room to room like a somnambulist while Bruce Silverman trailed behind, opening closets and demonstrating light fixtures. "The marble is all real, imported from Italy. As you can see, the whole place is very well appointed."

Claire did not appear to have heard and he changed tactics suddenly. Maybe he was scaring her off. Maybe she thought she couldn't afford it.

"Now, I'll bet you're thinking to yourself that this place is going to cost a pile. Well, I can tell you, the sellers are very, *very* motivated."

Claire's eyes swept the rooms. This is where Victor Mott lived, this is where he died. This was where *Peyton* lived. She had left this home to find another. . . .

"Can I see the nursery?" Claire asked.

Bruce smiled his salesman's smile. "How'd you know there would be a nursery? Heeey," he said, shooting her a sly look. "You've seen the house before, haven't you, you little sneak?"

Claire smiled tightly as he showed her into the nursery. It was as lavishly appointed a room as a new mother could ever dream about. Only one detail of this luxurious nursery matched Joe's far more modest room: a frieze of bright blue-and-green turtles that encircled the room. She stared hard at them for a moment, then turned away.

"Charming nursery, don't you think?" Bruce asked, but Claire had turned her attention to the Formica cabinets, stuffed with baby clothes, baby toys, baby accessories. Everything a baby would ever need. Claire could feel the yearning in these possessions, the desire and impatience of a soon-to-be mother. For a second she almost felt sorry for Peyton.

Then she caught sight of something that made her blood run cold. It was a pump with a clear plastic funnel, a very utilitarian object, out of place in this room full of soft pinks and blues.

"That's strange," said Bruce. "What kind of toy is that?"

Claire was transfixed. "It's not a toy. It's a breast pump."

"A breast pump?"

"A woman can use it to keep her milk up,

even when there is no baby to nurse." She felt sick to her stomach. Peyton had been nursing her baby, her nipple in his mouth. Joe had been receiving his nourishment, his life from Peyton's milk, not his natural mother's. She felt her gorge rising at the monstrousness of Peyton's actions and started for the door.

"Hey!" Bruce shouted. "Wait up."

Claire didn't stop. She hurried through the house and made for her car. She jumped behind the wheel and took off, the car screeching away from the curb.

Bruce Silverman stood on the sidewalk, looking after her, puzzled. No sale, he thought sadly.

CHAPTER 23

Claire sped across town, gripping the wheel. She watched the road but didn't really see it; her mind was spinning, but not out of control. It was clicking over like a machine, computing and analyzing.

It all made sense now. Peyton had mysteriously arrived on their doorstep. Claire dimly remembered being surprised, but Peyton had seemed so perfect that she hadn't thought twice about hiring her. She recalled that she hadn't even bothered to call any of the references Peyton had left.

But then the troubles had begun. The missing envelope containing her husband's precious work, Joe's refusal to eat. Claire's cheeks burned hot as she thought of the torment and pain Peyton had caused poor Solomon. How ashamed she felt! The moment Peyton was out of the house she would find him and try to make amends.

Like a flash, she realized that Peyton had made her suspect that her husband and her best friend were having an affair. She had planned Claire's humiliation at the party. Everything she had touched had led to mistrust and discord.

And to death. There was no way Peyton could have known that Marlene would discover the truth, no way she could have set the trap in the greenhouse for Marlene. That trap had been meant for herself, Claire. Peyton had emptied the inhalers. Peyton wanted her dead. Peyton wanted her family. . . .

She pulled into the driveway of the house just as Peyton was putting dinner on the table.

Michael jumped to his feet when she came into the dining room. He looked worried, but Claire felt more calm than she could remember being in a long time.

"Where have you been? I couldn't figure out where you could have gone. I called the Botanical Gardens."

Claire ignored him, her steely gaze fixed on Peyton.

"Are you all right?" Michael demanded.

Claire advanced on Peyton; their eyes locked together. She didn't notice that her husband and her daughter were looking at her as if she were an intruder in her own house.

"Claire? What the hell is going on?"

"Claire," Peyton said soothingly, "you look worn-out. Why don't you—"

Claire's lip curled and her arm pulled back. Without hesitation she let fly with her fist, her knuckles smashing into Peyton's face. Peyton flew backward, crashing into a chair and crumpling to the floor.

Emma screamed.

"You're fired!" Claire shouted.

"My God, Claire! What the hell is going on here?"

Claire advanced a step, her fists ready. She stared down at Peyton, sprawled on the floor, groggily raising her head. A thin trickle of blood ran from her nose and her lip was cut.

"She's been . . . plotting all along."

"Plotting?"

"She's Dr. Mott's widow, Michael."

Michael paled. "She's *what*?"

Fear gripped Peyton and she struggled to her feet. "Claire—"

"Get out of my house," Claire snarled.

Peyton looked from Claire's angry features to

Michael. "Michael . . . She's turning on me, just like you said she would."

"I *what*?"

"She doesn't realize how I've come through for this family. Tell her, Michael. She has to know sometime."

"Know *what*?"

"Know about what? Know about *us*, Michael. Tell her about us."

"*Us*? There's no us, Peyton." He took a step closer. "You have to leave. Now."

Hurt and betrayal shot through Peyton's clear blue eyes. She had crossed the line between reality and fantasy. "How can you say that, Michael?" Her voice was high and anguished. "What are you doing? You said there was only one woman for you, remember?"

Michael put his arm around Claire and gathered her to him. "I meant Claire. My wife."

Peyton shook her head quickly, like a boxer who has taken a rock-hard punch. Michael's words had hurt her more than Claire's blow. Then her face hardened. "Okay. Fine. I'll just get my baby and we'll be on our way."

"Baby?" yelled Claire. "Your *baby*?"

"I mean," she said calmly, "I'll just go down and get my things."

"Michael, I want her out. Now."

Michael nodded. He walked to the front door

and threw it open. It had started to rain. "You leave now, Peyton. We'll pack your bags and you can pick them up at the lab tomorrow."

Peyton nodded. "Michael," she said matter-of-factly, "you're right. That would be better for everybody." She picked up her purse on the hall table, then turned and was about to walk out into the rain when Claire stopped her.

"Peyton," she said. "Your keys."

Peyton nodded absently. "Of course." She pulled the keys from her purse and placed them on the hall table. She smiled pleasantly and looked from one face to another, then around the room, as if bidding it a fond farewell. "I'm sorry if I have caused you any trouble. You've all been so kind." She turned and walked out into the rain like a zombie.

Michael closed the door behind her and locked it.

Emma had hidden under the dining-room table the moment her mother had landed the punch in Peyton's face. When she heard the door shut, she rushed out and threw herself on her parents, whimpering, tears in her eyes.

"That's okay, honey, it's okay," said Claire softly. "Everything is okay now." She turned to her husband. "Michael, call the police."

"The police?"

"And we're going to stay in a hotel," Claire said firmly.

"Now, come on, Claire, let's calm down. We've got her keys. She can't—"

Claire was in no mood for arguing. "She's capable of more than you think. She set up Solomon. And she killed Marlene. That 'accident' was meant for me. Understand?"

Michael took less than a second to put it all together. "Right. Get the children's things together. I'll call the police."

Once he got the police on the line, Michael wasn't quite sure where to begin. He decided that he wouldn't start from the beginning and he couldn't bring himself to make a charge of murder against Peyton. He hemmed and hawed for a moment and then just asked that a squad car be sent to his house immediately. He felt certain he would be able to explain what was going on if he could do so face-to-face.

"We can't send someone immediately," said the police dispatcher, "not unless you have a life-threatening situation. Do you, sir?"

Michael hesitated a moment. "Uh, no," he said finally.

"Okay. We have your address, we'll send someone over the first chance we get."

Unsatisfied, Michael put down the phone, shaking his head. He walked from the kitchen into the dining room. Everything was just as they had left it. The chair was on its side on the floor, the casserole Peyton had cooked sat cooling on the table. Only a few minutes had passed since the drama had been played out in this room, but it seemed as if it had happened weeks ago.

He righted the chair, wondering if they weren't overreacting, if Claire hadn't transmitted her hysteria to the rest of the family. For a moment he doubted that Peyton could actually have done all the things Claire blamed her for.

Still, it was better to indulge Claire now, spend the night in a hotel, and sort everything out in the morning. He looked at the food on the table, wondering if he should tidy up a little. Then, with a wave of his hand, he dismissed the notion.

He started for the door but suddenly stopped, listening intently. Very faintly, somewhere in the house, he heard classical music.

He followed the sound into the kitchen. The radio on the counter was off. He stopped again and cocked his head. The music was coming from downstairs, from Peyton's room.

Michael opened the door. Standing at the top of the steep steps, looking down into the darkness, he felt his nerves tingling. The music was louder; it was definitely coming from down there. He faltered a moment at the top of the stairs, then took the first step down into the gloom.

Halfway down he stopped. "Peyton?" he called into the gloom. There was no answer.

He was at the bottom of the stairs now, in the laundry room that led to Peyton's lair. He glanced at the cellar door, the one that led directly into the yard, and saw that it was closed and locked. The door to Peyton's room was slightly ajar and a dim light glowed from within.

Michael cleared his throat noisily, as if warning whoever was within that he was outside. "Peyton?"

He took a deep breath and pushed open the door of the bedroom. It was empty. Music floated from the speaker of the clock radio and he quickly turned it off.

Smiling at his own fear, Michael walked quickly out of the room, snapping off the light as he went, and then started climbing the steps. Suddenly he felt as anxious as Claire to be out of the house. It was only his imagination, he knew, but he couldn't shake the feeling. Things would look better in the clear light of day.

Michael pulled open the door at the top of the stairs and had a split second to register the figure standing in the kitchen. It was Peyton, her hair plastered down to her skull by rainwater. She held a shovel in her hands and she swung it with powerful force, smacking him square in the chest.

Michael felt the rockets of pain all over his body, bright lights exploding behind his eyes. His legs buckled and he tumbled down the stairs, throwing his hands up to protect himself.

Mercilessly, Peyton advanced on him and swung the heavy iron shaft again, catching him in the side of the head. The sound of bone and teeth cracking seemed to fill his skull. Peyton hit him again and he toppled over the banister, falling ten feet to the concrete floor.

Peyton stopped for a moment to examine her handiwork. Michael was not moving and blood oozed from his jaw and temple. His right leg was doubled under him at an unnatural angle.

"Traitor," she spat.

Claire had thrown a few items into a valise and grabbed a couple of toys for Emma and a handful of diapers for Joe. As her eyes swept the nursery she hesitated, not quite sure of what to do next.

From downstairs came the sound of a door slamming. Claire ran to the upstairs landing. "Michael?" All was silent from the lower story of the house.

Panic was beginning to creep into Claire's voice. *"Michael?"*

"Mommy," said Emma pathetically. "I'm scared."

Claire turned to her daughter. "Emma. Go back into the nursery. Lock the door behind me and stay with Joe. Don't open up until I say. Understand?"

Emma nodded.

"Don't open the door to anyone but me, okay?"

"Yes," she said.

"Good girl." She squeezed her daughter tightly and closed the door, waiting until she heard the lock click. Then she started downstairs.

Nothing in the living room was out of place. The lamp next to the couch was still on. The only sound was the beating of the rain against the windows.

"Michael?" Her voice seemed very loud in the still house. She moved slowly, carefully, as if walking a tightrope or crossing a mine field.

Nothing had changed in the dining room except for the chair Peyton had knocked over. It was now back in its proper place. Claire couldn't recall having done it. Probably it was Michael, she thought.

The kitchen, too, was silent. A bundle of knitting—Peyton's knitting—lay on the table.

"Michael?"

The cellar door was open. Claire walked to the edge of the steps and peered into the darkness. In happier times, the cellar stairs had seemed innocuous. But now they seemed as inviting as a crypt.

Her heart pounding in her chest, blood roaring in her ears, Claire fought the urge to flee. Where was Michael? He might need her; she had to find him.

She started down the stairs, her guard up, ready to fight for her life. At the base of the staircase, surrounded by darkness and shadow, she squared her shoulders and summoned the courage to push open the door of Peyton's room when she felt a hand, cold and clammy, close around her ankle.

CHAPTER 24

Claire gasped and wheeled around, striking out in the darkness. Michael lay sprawled at her feet. His pants were dark with blood and his face pale with agony. Claire fell to her knees next to him.

"Michael! Oh, my God!"

"She's in the house," Michael gasped.

"Michael—"

"My leg is broken. We need help."

Claire stood up. "Hang on," she said. "I'm going to get the kids." She started up the stairs.

"Call the cops!"

At the top of the stairs Claire opened the door into the kitchen cautiously, fearing that Peyton was lying in wait. The kitchen was still and quiet. She crept toward the phone and snatched it off the wall. But before she could dial the number, the receiver was knocked from her hands by the edge of a shovel.

Peyton was standing there, weapon in hand, her eyes boring into Claire, her face a mask of hatred. She raised the shovel menacingly and advanced on her.

"You're in the way, Claire. This is my family now." Peyton swung her weapon at Claire's head. Claire dove for cover as the shovel smashed into a row of canisters, and flour and sugar exploded in a cloud of whiteness.

Claire scrambled to her feet and made a dash for the door, but Peyton cut her off, swinging the shovel again. This time the weapon smacked Claire squarely on the back of her head. There was a peel of thunder somewhere in the middle of her brain and she crumpled to the floor.

Grinning, Peyton threw the shovel aside and strode toward the staircase, determined to get her children and make her escape.

Upstairs, Emma had disobeyed her mother. She had heard the crash of crockery in the kitchen and had thrown open the door. Now she was standing uncertainly on the landing. Peyton found her there, fear and distress on her little face.

"Hi, sweetheart," she said lovingly. "Now, I don't want you to worry about a thing. Everything is going to be just fine. Now, just tell me where the baby is."

Emma stared at her balefully. She was afraid of the woman she had once loved.

"Come on," Peyton said sweetly. She knelt down until her face was level with the little girl's. "Tell me. Tell Mommy where he is."

Emma thought for a moment, then her shoulders slumped, as if in submission. She pointed through the nursery doorway. "He's in there."

"See? That wasn't so hard, was it?" Peyton's face softened and she stood up and walked quickly into the nursery. She bent over the crib. It was empty.

"Emma!" she snarled. She whipped around just in time to see the nursery door closing.

"You're not my mommy!" cried Emma, slamming the door and throwing her weight against it. She had the key in her tiny hand.

As Emma fumbled getting the key in the lock Peyton threw her body against the door. Just as she hit she heard the bolt slip home. Beating at the door with her fists, Peyton screamed at the top of her lungs, "Emma! Emma! You open the door right this minute. Emma, do you hear me?"

Emma took a step back from the door and

stared at it, panting. For a moment there was silence from the nursery. Then came a fearsome blow. Peyton had seized the poker from the fireplace set and was battering her way through.

Emma jumped at the sound and ran down the hall. She pulled open the linen closet. Nestled among the towels and the sheets was Joe, wrapped in his blanket. She glanced down the hall. The black iron head of the poker smashed through the wood again and again. In a matter of seconds Peyton would be free.

Emma jumped into the linen closet and closed the door. She crouched next to her little brother, holding him. She tried not to breathe.

The nursery door flew open and Peyton stood there, poker in hand. She charged down the hall and kicked open the door of the master bedroom.

"Where are you, Emma?" She quickly overturned the bed and swept through the closet, then charged into the bathroom and thrust aside the shower curtain.

Her jaw set with determination, she stalked into Emma's room and searched it thoroughly. There was no sign of the little girl. Downstairs. She had to be downstairs. . . .

At the top of the stairs she paused and listened. There was silence in the house—then she heard it. Very faintly, somewhere behind her, she heard Joe give a little cry. She turned triumphantly and stared at the linen-closet door, an exultant smile on her lips.

"Emma, you have been a very naughty girl." As she swept the door open her look of victory turned to one of pure fury. Resting among the linens was the baby intercom, the speaker filled with the sound of Joe's cries. Peyton snarled and grabbed the plastic box, angrily smashing it against the closet door.

The crying continued somewhere in the house. Peyton stood very still, listening, trying to locate the sound. It was not on that floor; nor was it downstairs. Very slowly, she raised her eyes to the ceiling. Emma was upstairs, in the attic.

Poker in hand, Peyton climbed the steep stairs and burst into the low-ceilinged, musty room. Her eyes grew wide when she took in the scene.

"You!"

Solomon stood at the high attic window, Joe in his arms, helping Emma out onto the rain-slick ledge beyond the opening. The shafts of Solomon's tallest ladder could be seen poking up into the window.

Solomon looked out. There was no way he could get them all out the window before Peyton attacked. He curled himself around Joe, turning his shoulder to his enemy. Peyton advanced on him, raising the poker.

"Give him to me," she hissed.

"No."

Peyton smiled nastily. "No?"

"No!" said Solomon firmly. "Y-you can't have him."

"Give me that baby or I'll bash your skull in!"

"You leave him alone!" Emma screamed.

"Peyton!"

Peyton turned. Claire stood in the attic door, a long, sharp carving knife in her hand. "Get away from him," she ordered.

"I told you you were in the way." Peyton marched toward Claire and without hesitation slashed out with the poker, catching the knife and throwing it far into the darkness of the room. The second blow caught Claire on the shoulder.

"Mommy!" shrieked Emma.

Claire sank to her knees and Peyton moved in for the kill, her poker lifted high above her head. Suddenly a terrible wheeze broke from Claire's lips and her chest heaved as she snatched desperately for breath. Peyton shook her head in disgust.

She lowered the poker, then bent down until

her lips were at Claire's ear. "What's the matter, Claire? Can't breathe?"

Claire's wheezes filled the room, her eyes wild with panic and pain.

"You are pathetic," Peyton spat. "When Michael makes love to you, it's my face he sees. When Emma cries out in the night, she calls my name. Your baby gets his milk from my breasts." She looked at Claire with pity. "You're all dried up, Claire. When the chips are down, you can't even draw a breath."

Claire was convulsing with the effort to breathe, her mouth opening and closing desperately.

Peyton stood and bore in on Solomon, the poker raised above her head. "Give me that baby or I'll kill you!"

"No!"

Behind her, Claire raised her head. Her gasping stopped and she stood, resolve replacing helplessness, her asthma attack a fake. Peyton looked over her shoulder and saw Claire leaping toward her, throwing her full weight against her.

Peyton was caught off balance and flew toward the window, crashing through the frame onto the ledge. She teetered there for a split second, her arms windmilling as she fought desperately to regain her balance. Then she toppled into the wet night sky and plummeted to the ground. Her fall was broken by Solomon's fence—two white slats spearing her in the back, her head thrown back, her eyes open to the rain that poured out of the black clouds.

"Mommy!" Emma threw herself into Claire's arms.

Solomon uncoiled from around the baby and showed him nervously to Claire. "D-don't w-worry, Claire," he said. "I didn't hurt him."

Claire nodded. "I know."

Solomon anxiously held out the baby to his mother. He knew that Claire didn't like him to have the baby in his arms. "You can take him now."

Claire shook her head. "No, I have to go help Michael. You take care of him."

"Me? Take care of him?" Solomon couldn't quite believe it.

"Why not?" Claire said with a smile. "You've done a good job so far."

Solomon beamed as she put her arm around him and kissed him warmly on the cheek. "Besides," she said, "you're family. . . ."

There's an epidemic with 27 million victims. And no visible symptoms.

It's an epidemic of people who can't read.

Believe it or not, 27 million Americans are functionally illiterate, about one adult in five.

The solution to this problem is you... when you join the fight against illiteracy. So call the Coalition for Literacy at toll-free **1-800-228-8813** and volunteer.

Volunteer Against Illiteracy. The only degree you need is a degree of caring.